Merseyside Tales

by

Michael Kelly

Print Origination (NW) Ltd
Formby, Merseyside

First published in 1993 by
Print Origination (NW) Ltd
Formby Business Park
Formby, Merseyside L37 8EG

© Michael Kelly

ISBN 0 903348 40 3

Typeset in Palatino by
Print Origination (NW) Ltd
Formby Business Park, Formby Merseyside L37 8EG
Printed and bound in Britain

Contents

Wapping Dock at the height of its usage. circa. 1907

The Good Neighbour

It was a quiet, uneventful day; the only movement outside of the small terraced house was the grey mist that rolled up the River Mersey on its journey from the Irish Sea. Seagulls and pigeons had gone to rest; even the sparrows clustered in little groups under the eaves of the roof. An overcoat of greyness was sweeping over the banks of the Mersey; it was Mother Nature's way of putting all life on the back burner. Most of the trees had shed their leaves, and the plants that lay around in the soil looked limp and tired. Had the window been open, the grey misty overcoat would have made its way into the warm, cosy room. But Billy had made sure that the window was securely closed to keep out the damp on this November day.

Billy was content as he looked out of the window. And why shouldn't he be? He had earned his retirement from the building trade. He looked pleased with himself as he sat in his easy chair, his broad hands going through the movements of lighting his pipe; his hands were still tanned just like his round, weather-beaten face.

A soft breeze gently touched the water of the River Mersey during the summer months and the salt air, and warm rays had given Billy's body the insulation it needed to get him through the first winter of his retirement. He puffed away, the smoke from his pipe covered most of his face, but the smoke could not hide the pale blue eyes that shone through the haze.

Billy's eyes looked up from his pipe, and again cast a look towards the window. He could see that the mist had left damp

1

streaks on the outer side of the glass. His blue eyes smiled and shone like a beacon as Billy gazed towards the cosy gas fire. He could see that one of the three radiants on the fire was broken. I had better be doing something to renew it, he thought. Mary, his friend and neighbour, had been at him for some time to get the fire in good working order.

"Speak of the devil" he said to himself. He heard the key going into the front door lock of his house, "that will be the little lady herself".

Billy's friend never ever knocked. She had the key to the house in order to take care of things whenever he was working away. Since his wife had died some years ago, Billy had lived alone. His children had either married, or had moved away.

"I see you've done nothing about that damn fire", said Mary, "Instead of sitting on your arse smoking that pipe, you'd be doing yourself a favour if you stripped that fire down and got it working properly. And while you're at it, get into town and change the broken radiant".

"Aye," said Billy with a tone that sounded like a man who had been caught shirking his work. "Mary" he said with a little meekness in his voice, "do you mind putting the kettle on, and we'll have a cup of tea, and then, I promise you, I'll get stuck into the job".

"You might be retired", Mary answered, "but you haven't lost the use of your arms and legs yet. Put it on yourself, I'm not your servant, nor your home help".

The tea made, they both sat drinking it whilst staring into the fire. Once again, Billy stoked up his pipe and struck four matches before he got the thing to light. Savouring the taste of his Erinmore tobacco, the scene was set for him to slip back into the tranquillity he had enjoyed before Mary had disturbed his solitude.

"Come on, for God's sake, do something with that fire. Those fumes are liable to lay you low forever".

Billy swore, and set to work dismantling the fire from a secure position in the hearth.

2

"Why don't you take the three radiants out first" Mary added, "or it will not be just one you'll have to renew, it'll be all three of 'em".

"Stop your nagging" growled Billy, "Why don't you leave me alone to get on with the job? Can't you see the damn fire's heavy and I'm having to wrestle with it? I can do without you going on, but if it satisfies you, I'll take them out".

Billy threw the broken radiant into the waste bin which stood at the left of the hearth and placed the other two on the floor.

"If you leave them sitting there on the floor, they'll get trodden on by those clumsy feet of yours" said Mary.

"Will you shut up woman", said Billy loudly, "before you walked in, I was enjoying the peace of me surroundings and me baccy on this, the first day of me retirement; you mean well woman, but sometimes you sound like a bloody nagging wife".

"If you don't get your head together man, yer retirement will be a short one".

"Don't be bothering me, the fire's out, and the job's being done, anyway, go and see who that is banging on me door. I hope to God it's not another one like yourself".

It was Tom, an old friend of Billy's who had come along to see how he was enjoying his first retirement day.

"Come in and sit down" said Mary, "as you can see Billy's busy".

"You seem to be enjoying yourself, Billy what are you doing with the fire?" asked Tom.

With a sarcastic tone Billy turned to Tom. "Well now, Tom, I've decided to turn the fire round, so that the heat from it goes up the chimney stack. I thought it would be a nice change to be able to look at the back of the fire".

Mary giggled, and Tom shook his head as Billy laboured laboriously. "Will the two of you clear off while I get meself ready for town", Billy requested.

Some hours later, Billy was back kneeling on the hearth reassembling the gas fire, and in walked Mary.

"Oh, I see you've nearly got the fire fixed back in position".

"Yes, Mary, yes you're quite right, I've nearly finished. Since you came here this morning giving yer orders out, I have had the time of my life. First I remove the monster from the hearth almost rupturing meself in the process. Then, I place the two good radiants on the floor, as instructed by yerself. While I was cleaning the chimney flue, the damned fire fell over, breaking one of the two good radiants that remained, leaving me with only one."

"So off I goes into town in the old banger car, with the one and only radiant that I had left. The precious radiant I placed on the passenger seat next to me – and away I went."

"Coming up to the traffic lights I braked and the radiant slides slowly to the edge of the seat, topples off and shatters into bloody pieces. Me first thought after that was to return immediately and strangle yerself."

"If I live to be ninety, I will always remember how you went out of yer way to make sure that I was kept very active on this, the first day of my retirement".

"It's not every man that is blessed with such a good friend and neighbour as yerself."

"Never mind the sarcasm, perhaps if you listen to me in the future you will live to be ninety" answered Mary as she put a light to the newly assembled radiants.

A Liverpool Street circa. 1896

The Stranger

In Liverpool City Centre, there are many fine buildings, and, deep in the base of one of these buildings, you would find the maintenance men whose job it is to carry out various jobs on the many services that run through the subterranean passages of the building.

During break times the men would make their way to the boiler house; this was an ideal spot for having a cup of tea and a sandwich, away from the prying eyes of the officials who worked on the upper floors of the Law Courts building.

The three characters had worked together in the passages for many years. Bobby Maguire always had more to say than the other two; he worked out all the problems that they encountered – domestic, work and political. Bobby was the expert whether right or wrong. Mick Manning was the joker and would always have a funny tale to tell. Then Johnny Nelson, who was the quiet one of the three, looking to Bob for the right answers, and to Mick for the laughter.

Mick was forever doing jobs *on the side'*. He was a good bricklayer and would had many amusing stories to tell – like the one about the old couple that employed him to rebuild part of their back-yard wall: the wall backed onto an entry that was just wide enough to allow a small vehicle to pass through. Mick called to start work on a Saturday morning. Talking to the old lady in the back-entry, she pointed to the post that held her clothes line; all the yards in the street had a long post sticking up from the wall, that backed onto this entry.

"Mick", said the little old lady, "I had a terrible shock

yesterday".

"You did?" said Mick, with a look of concern for her.

"You see that clothes line. Well, when I went out shopping, it was up and when I came back it was lying flat in the yard. I went out again and when I got back, it was back up again. I was beginning to think me marbles were loose when my husband told me that a man with a van with ladders on the top knocked all the clothes lines in the entry down and then came back and put them up again. Was I ever glad to know that."

Bobby would always go to the boiler house when it was time for the morning break: he would get there a couple of minutes before his two comrades to put the kettle on. As he entered on this particular morning a young man of about twenty five was sitting on his favourite part of the bench. He was a good-looking man, with a nice head of dark hair that had a blue sheen, where the rays from the light bulb struck the crown of his head. His face was round, with brown eyes, not unlike Bobby, but much younger.

Bobby wanted to speak to him, but decided against it until Mick and Johnny arrived. "Who is this *cowboy?*" thought Bobby – all strangers were 'cowboys' to Bobby, the young man sat in silence. Mick entered next, and looked first at the stranger and then at Bobby.

"Who's this Bob, a new start, or has he come to cadge a cuppa?"

"I don't know" said Bob, "You had better ask him yerself".

"Have they sent you down to give us a hand?", said Mick in a sarcastic manner, as he sat down next to the stranger.

Johnny was seated waiting for Bobby to pour the tea, he could not take his eyes off the stranger: being a quiet type, he was more sensitive to strangers.

"What are you doing here lad, have you got a job on?" asked Johnny.

"No," said the stranger, "I was just passing so I thought I would just come in and sit down".

"What do you mean, you was just passing", said Bobby,

"we're right down in the bowels of the building, and you were 'just passing'".

"I didn't mean I was passing the building outside, I was down here and saw your little boiler house, so I came in and sat down".

"You're not from around these parts are you? I thought there was something different about you" said Mick. Johnny was still sitting staring at the stranger. He was sure that Bob and Mick would get to the bottom of it.

"Do you take sugar in your tea lad?" said Bobby to the stranger.

"Thanks but I don't drink tea".

"I've never seen you down here before" said Johnny with his eyes still fixed upon the stranger.

"Well, I did work down here in the past".

"When was that?" asked Mick with a frown on his face.

"It was many years ago".

Looking at Bob, Mick raised a finger to the side of his temple, as if to indicate that the young stranger was a little retarded or had a screw loose.

"How could you have worked down here many years ago?" said Johnny. He and his two mates were in their forties, and the stranger was only a young man.

By now, everyone was seated and ploughing through their sandwiches, leaving the young man to look on. It was at break times that the men would focus on the great social problems of the world; when their stomachs were satisfied they could nourish and expound their own prejudices.

Men have been deliberating important issues for years, but these three could, within minutes, dissect the carcass and fill it with their own prejudice, creating in the process great confusion in their own minds.

"Bob", said Johnny, "you know in Russia; well the male ballet dancers learn to box to stop them from getting female tendencies because of the movement of the dance".

"No, you've got it all wrong" said Bob, "That's not the

reason they teach them to box. It's like this. In China they split the men from the women and put them all in separate communes, and that's what makes them gay. It's the same in Greece and Russia", continued Bob.

"I see," said Johnny, with a puzzled look on his face, but not daring to challenge Bob's brilliant analysis.

"I suppose you know your way around this building" said Mick to the stranger, in a snide manner. Johnny and Bob looked on and leaned over the table with their faces pushed towards the young man. The three characters waited for an answer to the question and the expression on their faces was like schoolboys waiting for an explanation in the classroom.

"Yes, I do know my way around this building" said the young man.

"You must have worked the night shift, after we had gone home," said Johnny, with a satisfied grin on his face, believing he had made a well thought out statement. He looked in the direction of his two comrades for approval.

"Well you know, I suppose you could say I have been on the night shift", said the young man.

Johnny's confidence was increasing with each minute. He continued to interrogate the stranger, "when did they let you out?"

"What do you mean?" said the young man, "When did they let me out?"

"Well, put it this way lad. You come in here and sit down, then you tell us you've worked on this building and now you say you've worked on the night shift, we don't work night shifts here".

"I know *you* don't", he said.

"You are a bit strange though" said Johnny.

"Why am I strange? Is it because you and your friends don't listen to what other people say?"

"It's not that" said Mick, "but you see we don't take easily to strangers down here".

"I can assure you that I am no stranger to this place".

"Prove it" said Bob.

"Are you sure that you want me to prove it?"

"If you can't, don't bother to come down here again," said Mick.

Then he looked at Johnny and Bob to make sure that *they* approved of his straight talk.

"Alright", said the young man. "I am what you would call a ghost".

Despite all their big talk, they were servile when confronted by anyone who had a clear-cut and sober appearance, but now, any respect that the three characters had for the young man, with his smart appearance, his clear command of the English language combined with his demure manner, had gone.

"A ghost is it, well then let's see you walk through the wall", said Johnny.

"Yes, and how about putting your head under your arm", said Mick.

Now it was the turn of Bob the thinker, "Listen lad, have they let you out for the day, or have they brought you to the Law Courts because you've been scaring them in the nut-house?".

"Why have you become so violent in your expressions towards me just because I told you that I am a ghost?. You always dismiss anything that you don't understand so that things that you have a little knowledge of become distorted. In your mistaken belief that you have an understanding of the importance of your knowledge in your world, your only achievement confusion in yourselves which you pass on to each other. If only you could stop and try to think about what you are actually saying. You would be far more understanding if you were prepared to listen to others sometimes. I have observed you for many years. You are good craftsmen, but you are immersed in your own petty little worlds".

Mick, Bob and Johnny were stunned by this barrage of criticism from the stranger. Mick slopped his tea down the front of his overalls.

Bobby regained his composure and continued to look at the young man "Tell me", he said "You say you have been here a long time, so tell us about yourself before you go, and make it quick, because we're going back to work in a minute".

"I was a Civil Engineer, working on this building when it was being built and I slipped and fell down a deep shaft and was killed, my body was never found.

"Do you think we're as daft as you?" said Bob.

Mick and Johnny were slapping their hands on the table and jumping up and down like idiots, making uncomplimentary remarks towards the stranger.

"Right," said Bob, "show us this shaft before you go. I can tell you now there is no shaft down here. If there was one, we'd know about it".

The young man led the way down the subterranean passages, they passed under the aches and arrived in an area that they had never been to before. There were no lights in the passages, the three comrades felt cold — more out of fear than anything else. They had stopped joking and kept looking at their young guide, their strange surroundings provoked fear and they now felt a lot more respect for the young man; their scornful attitude also had disappeared.

"This, my friends, is where I fell and died".

In front of them was a narrow shaft, not much wider than the average man. Even though there were no lights in this area, they could see into the shaft; it looked so deep and bottomless. The three men were very quiet; they gazed at their guide without comment, smiling now, the young man gained superiority.

Being the sensitive one, Johnny asked the stranger if they could go back.

"Certainly, I will guide you back".

Behind the young man, the three walked; the coldness of their unfamiliar environment slowly disappearing, the lights of the passages once more coming into view.

They were really glad to see the lights ahead of them, and also thankful when they were seated back in their little boiler house. The silence was still with them, as they sat motionless, all deep in their own thoughts, they could still feel the coldness of those dark passages, clinging to their bodies.

The scene in the boiler house was of three very dejected clowns, sitting on a wooden bench in the middle of a circus ring. Mick's long face, with his pointed chin reaching for the floor, his eye lids dropped, his vision directed towards the point of his chin, the joker was silent.

Bobby sat next to Mick, his head tilted to one side, his round face without expression, the mouth of his strong jaw hung loose, his heavy muscular shoulders leaned forward, but they were supported by the strength of his arms that had their elbows firmly into his knees. Johnny, the silent and sensitive clown, sitting with his elbows on the table, his head pushed back, his face lifted towards the ceiling, his blue eyes like empty pools without depth and no reflection coming from them. The fair hair on his head hung like yellow strands of weeds from the overgrown gutters on an old derelict house.

The comrades continued to sit, their bodies still motionless, their faces still blank, but in their minds they kept thinking about the young stranger, who had come among them. The young man had now gone, but things would never be quite the same in the subterranean passages.

They knew that they would never again find the dark cold passage, nor the young man who had been their guide.

Geoges Dock circa. 1895

13

Graduation Day

The presentation over, the Vice-Chancellor, a man with a cultured Irish accent, spoke of wisdom and knowledge: he quoted from Shakespeare and he had a profound affect on Tom.

It was a bright, sunny summer's day. Tom stood with his mother and grandfather in a little garden on the university campus: one of the nicer spots, he thought, this beautiful garden in the city that he called home. Tom's thoughts were already turning to places beyond the city that he loved. The sun was shining in this month of July and the garden was blooming, but, the city that he loved so much was in a state of decay.

Tom stood close to his mother and grandfather, while his friends took photographs of them, for a few seconds his mind wandered back to the day he gave up his job in the motor trade: a secure but poorly paid job in a city that was sinking economically. He was thinking too about all the dead-end jobs that he had tried since he had left school, at fifteen years of age.

They remained standing together on the grass of the park, his mother and grandfather were very proud of Tom's B.A. Degree: his mother kept looking up into his face, and only looked away when she was required to look into the camera. Tom was tall and Maria, his mother, was only three or four inches shorter than him. She was a woman of fifty eight but still retained the full figure of a woman twenty years her junior. Her hair was still fair, the years of discipline and

14

dedication as a professional dancer had rewarded her with good health and a youthful face.

Tom's thoughts were still focused on the five years since he had left his job. It only seemed like yesterday since he had left for Harlech in Wales to join a hundred or more mature students who were all keen to get a diploma in higher education over the next two years. He thought about the friendships that he had made during the two years at Harlech. But those friends had been scattered to the wind: only a few friendships had survived, but they would remain for the rest of his life.

Tom could feel the solid, but gentle frame of his mother's shoulder, as he stood with one arm round her, keeping her close to him; his other arm had a firm hold on his grandfather's frail shoulder. The old man was eighty one and Tom could feel the frailty of him, but he was thinking about the time when those shoulders were strong.

His grandfather had worked all his life without asking much as a reward: being able to give a service to the community was all that he had required. Tom could remember him when his back was straight and limbs were firm. His mind was not on the camera as he looked towards this man he was so proud of. As he held him, Tom felt that the strength of the old man's body was being transferred to him: his agile brains were being bequeathed to him. He knew that the gifts that he was receiving from his mother and grandfather – contained in the genes through reproduction – were far greater than all the material things in life; these things were left behind at death.

The old man was content and felt at rest with the world; this was one of the happiest days of his life. His mind was not only on Tom and his daughter; his thoughts were also on the streets that they had walked down on the way to the university. He could see that many of these streets had been swallowed up to become part of the university campus. He smiled as he stood with his family in the beautiful little garden that was surrounded by the high, ornate Victorian railings; once this garden was a place where only the rich would dare to enter. When his daughter spoke, he was still locked in his thoughts. Gently, she took his arm and pointed towards an iron seat where he could rest.

Maria watched her father walk over to the seat. No sooner had he sat down than one of Tom's friends walked over to take his place and had her photograph taken with himself and his mother. Maria wondered if she should join her father on the seat and allow another one of Tom's friends to stand by his side for the benefit of the camera. But Tom insisted that she remain where she was, by his side. Maria stood alongside her son and could hear the click of the camera. As she looked towards it, the camera was able to capture the gentle smile on her face. The camera, though, could not look into her mind as she allowed it to roam down the years, to a time in her life when she was at the crossroads; a young mother with a young baby, what would be their future? Whatever road she took, whatever decision she made, it had to be the right one for her son and herself. She had watched him grow from the helpless infant in the early years; from the foal with uncertain legs into the stallion with firm and strong legs. Yes, she could remember the times he had looked back at her with uncertainty in his eyes, as he moved further away to explore the world about him. Maria had known that she could only guide him, while he remained within the confines of her own influence. She remembered the doubts and fears that she had had over the years. Now, her son had mastered the art of coping with the world she had brought him into. Today, she felt very proud to be a mother.

Looking away from the camera towards the Victorian iron seat, she saw her father: Tom Senior had stoked up his pipe and contentedly puffed away on it. She could see that he was relaxed, sitting on the seat, with the gentle rays of sunshine covering his face. Maria could also see the smile which came from his eyes, as he puffed at his pipe. Words did not have to pass between them; they both knew that this young man had made this day, and their lives, worth living.

Memories of an Exile

The little man was sitting on a wooden box, watching the passengers disembark from the boat which had just arrived after a night-crossing from Dublin. Many seemed excited at the thought of seeing Liverpool for the first time; most people seemed happy and gave you the feeling that they knew where they were going. But the little old man, sitting on the box, looking at the happy people was thinking about the time he also was a passenger landing in Liverpool, after an awful night-crossing on the cattle boat. He was deep in thought, contemplating the happy, well-dressed people rushing off to all the different destinations which had already been arranged before they left Dublin for England. Whilst the old man sat watching and wondering, a smile spread over his face.

A young man of about twenty, stood looking at the old man sitting on the box. The young man was alone, "excuse me, sir", he said as he approached the old man sitting on the box, "Do you live in Liverpool?"

The old man came out of his thoughts, looked at the young man and replied, "Yes, I have lived in this town a long time".

"How long is that, sir?", said the young man.

The old man did not answer, he just sat and smiled at the young man.

"Then may I ask, sir, how old you are?"

"Yes, you may ask, I am three generations old".

"But how can you be three generations old, sir?", said the young man.

"Because I was born in 1843 in a little house in Carrigaline in

17

the county of Cork, and I travelled with my parents to Liverpool in 1847 and have been here ever since.

The young man looked at the old man, who was still sitting
on the wooden box and his gaze contained a sadness and compassion for his elder companion.

The old man looked straight into the eyes of the young man,
"No, I am not confused, I really am three generations old. I
once stood where you are standing now, after stepping off the
boat with my parents. I was four years old and I can still
remember the bundles of old clothes that they carried in their
worn hands. When we moved away from the docks we had
nowhere to live; as was the fate of many of us Irish who came
to England at that time. Now you are a well-fed young man,
with fine clothes and I wonder if you have ever given a
thought to your fellow countrymen, who were exiled in this
town. Would you like to see where my family went to live; it is
only a short distance from here?"

"Yes, I would", said the young man, knowing he still had
lots of time before he caught the London-bound train.

As they walked together, he noticed the large warehouses
that were busy with the trade of stacking and stowing goods
going to or from the ships. Queuing up outside of the
warehouses were many horse-drawn carts and wagons,
waiting to unload or load their cargoes. The young man
thought it was strange to see so many horse-drawn vehicles.
The thought crossed his mind that it was now 1982, and even
in Dublin itself, there were no longer any horse-drawn
wagons. Then he noticed another young man around the same
age as himself standing in the doorway of a warehouse dressed
in unfamiliar clothes. In fact, this person looked like a younger
version of the old man.

The young man turned to the old man and said "that that
man standing in the doorway there bears a strong resemblance
to yourself is a relative of yours?"

The frail old man just looked at the young man with the
same silent countenance as before, and with the same smile

18

that had induced the young man to approach the quaint little figure at the dockside. The young man then asked the old man if he would mind if he went and spoke to the man in the warehouse doorway.

"It is impossible for you to go and speak to that young man in the doorway".

"But why?", said the young man.

"Well, you are a stranger to that man and he would not relate to you".

"But I don't understand", said the young man.

"You will one day", said the old man, "When you are three generations old".

The young man looked at the old man; again with a look of compassion in his eyes. His frail friend led him on through the strange streets of Liverpool.

After a short time, the old man said: "This is where my family came to live when I was just four years old".

The young man found himself walking into a courtyard, but not the type of courtyard that housed the landed gentry of the past. This courtyard had little narrow houses, on all four sides, with a little narrow passage to gain entrance to the yard. The houses were so narrow that they looked as if they had been pushed together by two huge fists. Altogether, there were eighteen houses. In the middle of the courtyard, was a *"stand-pipe"*, with people drawing water from it.

The young man asked the old man why the people were drawing water from the pipe.

"It is because they have no water in the houses and this pipe is their only means of obtaining water it is only turned on for one hour, twice a day".

He noticed there were many people standing outside of the houses, and was about to ask the reason when the old man looked at him and said.

"You have a long way to travel with me, through three generations, and much to learn, these people live in houses with such tiny windows which let in so little fresh air through the house and when the fresh air does manage to come in, it is soon swallowed into those hungry lungs of the many people who live crowded in the houses. That is why they stand outside when the weather is warm enough".

"I notice that all the people have Irish accents I could almost be back in Irlend?"

"Again, young man, you have many things to learn: a chameleon may change its colour many times, but he will always remain a chameleon. Come with me now, and I will show you where I lived when I was a young man".

They continued, the young man walking alongside his frail companion. He now noticed that the streets were not quite as strange, or as dirty, as when they were walking past the warehouses.

"This is where I lived as a young man", said the old man, breaking the silence.

"Oh, I see", said the young man, "It is called Dublin Street?"

"Right", said the other.

When they turned into the street, the young man could see two blocks of tenements with open landings and a stairway in the middle leading to each landing. The old man kept looking at the young one, as if expecting a change of expression to appear on his face.

The young man turned to his elderly friend and asked: "Sir, why is it I see people who resemble you so much?"

The old man just smiled as the young man added: "Look up there on the second landing, I can see a middle-aged man who resembles you".

"You will understand soon", said the old man, still smiling.

"You keep telling me that I will one day understand, but sir, you can be no more than eighty five years old, and yet you say that you were four years old in 1847. If that were so, you would be now a great age indeed."

"I see that you can think for yourself", said the old man with a mischievous little smile, enlivening his withered face.

Now the young man was more than a bit confused and said to the other "You say that you are three generations old, but as far as I am aware, a person can live but one life".

"That", replied the old man, "is because unlike the chameleon, you will forget what you are, and where you come from".

"But sir," said the young man, "Like me, you are trapped inside one generation".

"No longer am I trapped" said the old man "for like the chameleon, I now remember quite clearly what I am, where I came from and, more importantly, why I came to a city lying on the opposite side of the Irish Sea".

The pair continued walking and a few yards further on, the old man stopped and turned to his companion: "This is where I live now. Please go on into the flat: the door is open and I shall follow you in after I have had a quick word with my neighbour".

The young man entered, nodding to the old man. After spending a little time in the flat, he noticed three framed photographs, placed on an old mahogany sideboard. Two of the three photographs were obviously taken many years ago and were faded, but the third, which must have been taken in recent years, was of his old friend.

At that moment, he turned and standing in the doorway was a middle-aged lady who said "Are you a relation of the old gentleman?"

The young man replied: "No, but we met a little earlier and he wanted to show me his home".

With a puzzled expression on her face, the woman said "The old man is dying in my flat and he is mumbling that he is three generations old".

The young man looked back at the photos and walked out of the flat.

The "Good Old Days"

The Midwife

Maurice felt very relaxed and happy as he walked through the village. He paused to look up at the sign over the little cafe. "What a quaint name", he thought, 'The Tiny Tea Shop'. "Can this really be the place, or have I got the address wrong?"

"It is true", Maurice thought to himself, "Have I really arrived, is this the house that my Grandfather lived in all those years ago?"

The questions kept coming to his mind and he tried to keep them in order, his mind was racing, his excitement mounting. "Calm down man!" Maurice said aloud to himself.

Maurice looked around the brightly decorated room. The ceiling was painted white and the walls emulsioned in magnolia. Hanging in the centre of the ceiling was a brass lamp. Maurice had to look with intensity to see if the lamp was powered by electric power and not oil.

Four round tables, with gingham covers, filled most of the room. On the hearth stood a gas fire, where once an open fire on a cold winter's night would have been the focus of attention. At the far side of the room, sitting at one of the little tables, was an elderly lady, she lifted her head when she heard the door open, gave Maurice a friendly smile, then looked down into her tea-cup.

Maurice was still standing and had not selected a table to sit at.

"Can I get you anything, Sir?"

Turning, he saw a dark-haired young man.

"Can I help you?"

23

"Oh, yes," said Maurice. "Could I have a pot of tea and a cheese sandwich please".

"Certainly, I'll not be more than a few minutes. My wife has just put the kettle on."

With a friendly smile the young man continued, "We don't have many customers first thing on a Monday morning".

"That's alright", replied Maurice, "I am on holiday, so I have plenty of time, as a matter of fact I am looking up old names and addresses. I am trying to trace some of my ancestry. Part of my family came from Cobh and settled in Liverpool, the town where I was born."

The young cafe owner seemed to show a polite interest in Maurice's quest.

"It would appear from the information I have that my grandfather was born in this very house", said Maurice. The young man appeared to be a little puzzled at Maurice's remarks. "This sounds very interesting", he said, "I must tell my wife, I'll just give her your order".

Maurice sat down and watched him disappear into the back room. He wondered whether the young man had thought him foolish, standing there talking about his grandfather.

"Ah well, I suppose a middle-aged man standing here talking to a stranger about his grandfather does sound a little foolish".

Maurice felt very content sitting in the small room – a room that his grandfather would have sat in all those years ago. The cafe was one of a number of small terraced houses; it was probably more or less the same as it was when his grandfather had lived in it. He continued to absorb every detail of the room, thinking how nice it would be if he could look over the rest of the place, and how interesting it would be to walk around what had once been his family home.

"I knew your grandfather", said the old lady, sitting in the corner of the room. Maurice was startled by the remark, for he had paid little attention to her, in case he was intruding on her privacy. He sat in disbelief, looking at the smiling woman.

"I am sorry if I startled you Maurice, but I did know your grandfather".

As if in a trance, Maurice continued looking at the old lady. "I suppose that you think I am just a senile old woman. Well you would be quite wrong". Maurice did not answer. For the first time he had a good look at the woman, who had thrown his mind into confusion. She had dark hair, despite her age; her hands were slim and her fingers long. He saw that she was wearing a dark blouse, with a narrow collar, with a row of very fine buttons running down the middle of the garment; a navy-blue shawl covered her shoulders; a long skirt fell loosely to her ankles; her feet were in leather lace-up boots.

"How could she know my name", he thought, "Perhaps I introduced myself when I spoke to the young man, when I entered the cafe. Yes, that must have been it".

Without wanting to offend the old lady, Maurice asked in a gentle voice, "How could you possibly know my grandfather? He would have left this house in the early part of the century".

"Oh, but I did", said the old lady, "You see Maurice, he left this house the year I departed your world". "All my life I lived in this house, until I died in very tragic circumstances".

By now Maurice had forgotten his surroundings and his mind and thoughts were focused only on the old lady.

"Would you like to tell me how you came to die?"

Maurice was shaken by what he had said, a cold feeling seemed to run down his spine.

"Yes, I will tell you", came a quick and firm reply. "The day I died had been a long and tiring one for me. I was the unofficial midwife with two expectant mothers to attend to that day and I saw two lovely children come into the world.

I retired to the room just above the one we are sitting in, we had no electricity or gas in those days, only paraffin lamps or the open fire. I made my way up the stairs, with my paraffin lamp and placed it on a small table that I had by the bedroom door, unfortunately, I had not put the lamp into the middle of the table, but near the edge – something I would not have done if I had not been exhausted. As I turned away from the table, I knocked the lamp with my arm and it burst into flames, a sheet of flame shooting up the door of the room. Soon, the room was engulfed in smoke. I could hear people outside, trying to get to me, but the flames spread throughout the room within seconds, trapping me forever".

Maurice was sitting motionless when he felt a hand on his shoulder. The young man had returned with his order.

"Are you alright?" said the young man.

Maurice looked up and smiled at the cafe owner, but the smile only conveyed a look of fear in Maurice's face. A tray had been placed on the table in front of him, holding the tea and sandwich he had ordered. Again, the man asked if he was alright.

"You don't look too well", said the young man, "Here, let me pour you some tea". Without waiting for a reply the young man was pouring from the pot, Maurice sat without protest.

"Drink it down, you will feel better".

There was concern in the man's voice. Maurice looked over to where the old lady had been sitting. She was no longer there, just an empty chair.

Standing next to the cafe owner was a fair-haired young woman, in her early thirties. It was clear for all to see that she was in the latter stages of pregnancy.

"My husband, Peter, has just been telling me about your grandfather. I would like to know more It sounds fascinating".

The young woman showed a growing interest in Maurice.

"Would you like to come into the back room, it's more comfortable".

Without protest, Maurice followed his young hostess.

"Sit yourself there, and make yourself comfortable".

The young woman pointed to a large easy chair. Maurice sat back in the chair. Peter and his wife were kept busy in and out of the kitchen, and left Maurice to his thoughts. Maurice went on thinking about his experience in the cafe. "Did I imagine all that took place in the next room? If I tell this young couple about the old woman they would think I was having a breakdown. Must be my mind playing tricks on me. Yes, that's what it must be, the idea of going back in time when I entered this house".

After a lull in their work, Peter and his wife joined Maurice in the kitchen. "I don't suppose your name would be Doyle?" Maurice said to the young couple, "You see that was the name of my grandfather, Maurice Doyle, the same as myself".

"No," said Peter "It's Sheils and my wife is Mary".

The young woman smiled at Maurice, "Now Maurice, that would be too much of a coincidence".

"Yes, you're right", said Maurice.

"I was a little concerned", said Peter, "For when I went back into the cafe earlier on, you seemed deep in thought, staring into the corner of the room, with there being no-one else in the room it made your anxiety more noticeable".

What had happened to Maurice in the other room came flooding back to him. "Will you stay for a spell", said Mary "And tell us all about yourself and your grand-parents?"

"Yes, I would love to stay a while", said Maurice, but he could not detach his mind from what the old lady had been saying to him.

Mary seemed glad to have someone to talk to. She was expecting her first child within the next day or so. A few years earlier, the young couple had bought the house and obtained planning permission to turn part of it into a cafe. They talked to Maurice long into the day, despite the interruption of the odd customer. He enjoyed the company of the bright and friendly pair, and talked freely of his family history, which had centred around Cobh.

"Will you stay the night Maurice?" asked Mary. "You're on holiday, so there is no reason for you to leave tonight".

Before Maurice could answer, Mary continued – "You can come and have a drink in the bar down the road later, with

Peter and I".

"Right, you've talked me into it", he grinned.

The bar was a homely place. Gradually the main room became packed with people. Maurice was the only stranger in the bar, and his Liverpool accent was of interest to some of the other customers.

"I have enjoyed myself this evening", Mary said to him.

"Normally, I would have been in bed by now. At the end of a day, I am usually worn out. But it won't be long now. Soon, it will be over", she smiled, tapping herself on the stomach.

Peter was talking to a man who had just entered the bar. The man was talking in a low voice. Peter turned to Mary.

"I won't be long. Stay here with Maurice, I'll be back in a few minutes". Mary knew by the sound in Peter's voice that something was wrong. Peter disappeared through the door. Obviously worried, Mary turned to Maurice. "Maurice, will you go and see if Peter is alright?"

Outside, people were running up the road. He ran with them and found Peter standing outside of the cafe, in a state of shock. Smoke and flames poured from the cafe. Peter turned and looked at him.

"Maurice, it's as well you came today. Had you not shown up, my wife would have been in that room".

Maurice could hear the voice of Peter as he offered his gratitude to him for turning up. But, Maurice's eyes and thoughts were firmly fixed upon the window over the cafe that was belching smoke and flames – and was almost certain he could see a figure inside, but later it was discovered no person perished in the fire.

Cartwright Place Liverpool 1926

The Prize Fighters

Tom was sitting on the long bench with his back to the wall: he liked to sit in the same spot every night, as it gave him a chance to see what was going on at the bar, sitting with him were his two friends, Mick and Danny.

Danny was a man of about sixty-seven years, and stood about five feet eight inches tall. He still retained a lot of the solid frame that was his trademark when he was a younger man. The pull of the fight game and the Boxing Ring had been felt by Danny when he was very young. In fact, Danny was only fourteen years old when he first stepped into the prize ring, in a Boxing Booth. The passing years had not diminished Danny's passion for his sport: those of his friends who sat around the table knew that the only thing that mattered to him, apart from his family, was his love of Boxing.

Danny was feeling a little nostalgic, but this mood was interrupted when he caught sight of his right ankle, which had swollen up and which was starting to look like a ripe peach.

Mick was quick to notice Danny's look of concern. "You make sure you get to the doctor in the morning, Danny" he said in a commanding voice.

Tom, with a little smile on his well-worn face nodded his approval, by dropping his head from the left and bringing it round to the right in a forty five degree angle, just the way he would have done in the old days as a young man doing his neck exercises. Unlike Danny, old Tom had taken a few too many punches in his younger days. Whenever you tried to engage Tom in conversation, he would merely smile and nod.

Tom was eight years younger than Danny and had a smaller frame. Any evidence that he had been an old prize-fighter had gone from his body. He was much slower than his friends, Mick and Danny, but his eyes still had the sparkle of his youth.

Mick continued to lecture Danny about his ankle.

"Now don't you forget Danny, you make sure you get to the doctor in the morning, or else there will be trouble between you and me".

Mick was always concerned about the welfare of his two friends and they usually took some action to eradicate their problems when Mick laid the law down. Mick was a smart little man of fifty-eight years. His boxing exploits had done him no visible harm. He was a good electrician and was still working at his trade. Because he was such a smart dresser, his old comrades loved to tease him by asking if he had just been to a wedding or funeral.

"I've had a good night in the Gym" said Danny, "I've got some promising kids and will get some champions out of them".

For the last two years, Danny had been building a gymnasium; it was now filled with young men from eight to twenty years old. People were compelled to listen to Danny when he spoke about his young charges. Conviction and sympathy directed his work with them: he was going to pull them up by their bootlaces, make them into proud young men. Danny believed that the confidence found by Boxing would enable them to earn a living as pro-boxers, or any other occupation they might choose. Danny was convinced that the discipline of boxing would provide the determination necessary for climbing out of the abyss of unemployment, which prevailed in his beloved city of Liverpool. Building the gymnasium had given Danny a fresh purpose in life. Since the death of his wife, Danny had been very lonely. His children were either married, or had moved away to shape their own lives.

"Danny, how do you feel about those doctors who want to

ban boxing, on the grounds that it causes brain damage?" asked one of the bar locals.

"Brain damage" said a very indignant Danny. "They don't know what they're talking about. Do I look punchy and what about dapper Dandy" he was pointing to Mick. "No-one could accuse him of having brain damage". Looking towards old Tom, Danny paused. Tom looked intense, but managed a little smile. Danny failed to make any comment about him.

"One hundred and forty fights from fourteen to thirty-four, and I earned every penny. The college boys think they know it all, but I tell you, when you are born in a gutter, you have to learn to use your hands, or your feet, and anything else you have got to survive in that jungle out there. We don't all get the chance to use our brains the college way. It must be nice to be a medical man or a professor, spouting about brain damage. They don't know what they're talking about. Most of the lads I went to school with never had a glove on, and they had brain damage long before they were thirty. If you tried to talk to them about the arts, music, or theatre or a good book, they would just sit and grin like nut- cases. Their brains were slowly beaten to death, beginning from the day they were born. Poverty and stagnant life damaged their brains. Most kids will still have their brains smashed in by the sheer hopelessness of their lives". Danny went silent, hoping that his outburst had not sounded like a lecture, to his friends in the bar.

"You're right" said Mick.

Tom also gave a smile of approval.

They knew Danny always liked the chance to defend his sport and his way of life. His lifestyle had given him a chance to see new horizons, and meet people from many different circles. Danny's quick brain had not only absorbed punishment, it still had the capacity for knowledge.

Danny started to rub his swollen ankle. Mick was shaking his head with the thought of Danny in pain, knowing that he could have visited his doctor a couple of days earlier. Danny caught Mick's expression and was waiting for a gentle scolding from him, but Mick remained silent.

Thinking of the past, Danny decided to recount the time he had boxed on the same bill as the great Benny Lynch. His four friends had often heard the story, but they were patient with Danny and allowed him to proceed. Danny always recalled his younger days when he was feeling down.

"I have seen Benny Lynch knock a man out with one blow", said Danny, "When Lynch became famous, he knocked himself about with the booze, but I have watched him get knocked from one side of the ring to the other for five or six rounds. During those rounds he would be observing his opponent's footwork, the position of his hands, the movement of his body from the waist up to his head, the way he would slip away from punches. All this information was fed to the brain; the battle lines would be drawn-up like a game of chess. He would wait for his opponent to move into the right position, then Benny Lynch would become the master and he would strike out, felling his opponent motionless. Some people may call that brute force, but that would be wrong; only a genius like Benny Lynch could do that. The same man could measure speed and movements with his eyes".

By the time Danny had finished his tale, old Tom had slipped away and was heading home to his lonely little bed-sit.

Mick was rising from his chair, making ready to depart, "Good night, Danny. I'm off" he said.

His old friend was too engrossed in the past to notice the departure of his two old comrades. Mick and Tom had gone, leaving Danny with his memories.

The following night, Danny was missing from the bar.

"Good evening to you Tom" said Mick as he sat down next to his old friend. "I can see by the look on your face that Danny will not be calling in tonight". Tom gave him a half smile as with a slight nod of his head to Mick's comment, "It must be that leg of his".

"What's that you're saying, Tom?"

"I was thinking it must be his ankle still playing him up. Nothing else would keep him away, unless he has given up the ghost and somebody is laying him out this very minute, making him ready for the shroud".

"Now that's a nice thing to be saying about your best friend, and him probably laying there in agony with that ankle of his. It's as well, Tom, that he is not here now listening to you", said Mick, with a twinkle in his eyes as he turned his head to look straight into the face of Tom.

It was good to see Tom in a happy frame of mind: his moods of silence had increased over the last few months, much to the despair of his two comrades, Mick and Danny, for they, more than most people, had noticed the change in Tom's mental and physical appearance. The smile that spread across Tom's face when he realised he had amused Mick, cast away some of the shadows that had engulfed it in the last few months; it allowed Mick, for a few brief seconds, to see the countenance that he remembered in their younger days.

"How the years had passed", thought Mick. Like only yesterday it seemed, when he had sat and watched Tom move around the boxing ring, like a young Nel Tarleton. Nel was the British Featherweight champion in Tom's younger days.

"Mick, are you still working at your trade?" asked Tom.

The question startled Mick and brought him back from memory lane. "Yes, yes, Tom, I'm still at the trade, but things are not looking too good at the moment with the depression, or lack of opportunity, as some people choose to call it. Anyway, Tom, you're in a very talkative mood tonight. I'm glad to see you like this, it's a change from listening to Danny going on about the state of the world".

"Do you think he will be alright Mick?".

"Do you mean Danny?"

"Yes of course I do. Will he be alright?"

Mick could see that his old friend was becoming agitated.

"If it makes you happy, I will call on him tonight, when I am making my way home".

Mick's decision to take some positive action to make sure that Danny was not alone and suffering seemed to please Tom, who stretched his two arms to allow his hands to cover his knees and at the same time hunch his shoulders as though he was easing the pressure on his muscles. Tom was now content and oblivious to what was taking place around him. He did his stretching exercises, as he would do in his younger days, waiting for the next round. While Mick was concerned about Danny's health in recent weeks, he was more disturbed with Tom's more frequent moods of silences and lapse of memory.

Unlike Danny, Mick was not concerned for the rights or wrongs of the world; what mattered most to him were his friends and his trade as an electrician. It was only on rare occasions that Mick could be drawn into any sort of reminiscence of his boxing exploits. Tom's deteriorating health induced him to allow recollection of those early boxing days.

Although Mick was the younger of the prize fighters, there was little that he did not know about his two friends, or they about him. Tom's father was a big man with a square head and very little brain. He would lecture Tom on the benefits of being able to defend himself; any protests at not wanting to be a pugilist would be brushed to one side. Despite his background, Tom was bright and a very capable athlete, who mastered most sports. The very sport that Tom rebelled against in his young life was to be the one that he mastered above all others: beginning in those childhood days, boxing became his one and only true love, but in his passing years, it had deserted him.

Tom looked towards Mick. "What are you thinking about Mick? You're sitting very quiet".

"Oh, it's nothing very important. I was just thinking about the old days".

Tom seemed reassured and sat back in his seat, facing the bar to survey the scene in front of him: he got a lot of pleasure watching the coming and going of friends and strangers alike. When the bar was clear of customers for a few minutes, the bar staff would pass the time of day with Tom and his comrades. There was one dark-haired, busty girl who would often give Tom a special little smile and a wink with her big blue eyes. Danny and Mick would derive pleasure from watching Tom's face light up when he got a wink from his favourite barmaid, for they knew that a smile from this pretty young girl would turn Tom's mind to his youth. Not only did this pleasant young girl have the same name of Tom's first girlfriend, when he was sixteen, but the resemblance was also striking. Tom's two friends knew the sort of memories Elizabeth would evoke in him. Elizabeth had started school on the same day as Tom: they lived only a few doors away from each other. Often, Tom would recall to his two life-long comrades how he would sometimes walk along the canal bank with Elizabeth – the stinking canal which ran along the back of their houses: the canal ran along the back of the hovels they lived in along with the rats that were as big as some of the neighbourhood cats.

The Leeds Liverpool canal was very much a playground for Tom and his friends. Most of Tom's friends would strip off completely, plunge into the canal and so learn to swim. Tommy Smith's first encounter with the murky waters of the Leeds & Liverpool canal was a frightening experience. When he was nine years of age, he was taken by the hand and led to the water's edge. Slasher Smith, his father, made him undress, exposing the frail body of his son. After removing his own clothes, except for his battered trousers, he lifted Tom above his head and flung his young son into the middle of the stinking canal, as he would a dead cat. This crude method of teaching Tom to swim had been demonstrated in the past by Slasher Smith, when he had taught Tom's elder brothers to swim. Tom's body hit the water. Slasher followed his young son into the slimy water and proceeded to swim around his son. Flailing his hands in the water, Tom attempted to keep himself afloat with Slasher shouting words of encouragement. Round and round his father would swim, like an old porpoise, pushing the young boy back to the surface every time he started to submerge. Tom was not allowed out of the water until he could swim. Tom, like his elder brothers, left the water eventually, knowing that when he again entered the murky canal water, there would be no fear of him drowning, he would be just as competent a swimmer as the rest of the neighbourhood kids.

Elizabeth's parents were very determined that their daughter would not continue her friendship with Tom: they were completely against their daughter having any sort of relationship with a boy who had taken up boxing as a sport. Her parents moved away from the district, and Tom never saw Elizabeth again. Throughout his youth and manhood, he never had a serious relationship with a woman.

"Well, I think I'll be off", said Tom, "I've had enough for one night. It's been a bit miserable without Danny being here, don't you think so, Mick?"

"Oh, I see, my company is not good enough for you" said Mick, "Just because your old pal, Danny, is not here".

"Now it's not that I don't enjoy your company Mick, but you know it's always nice to have Danny sitting here with us".

"Yes, I understand Tom, I've missed Danny just as much as you have tonight, but don't worry about it old friend, I'm sure he will be hobbling through that door tomorrow night".

"I hope so", replied Tom.

"Do you mind if I walk back with you to your place, and you can make me a nice cup of coffee before I make my way home?" asked Mick.

Entering Tom's bedsit, Mick saw many mementoes of his boxing exploits. Hanging on the wall were a number of photographs, one being of the only woman that Tom was devoted to, his Mother. She was small and gentle, and had a great humility, despite being married to someone as ignorant as Slasher Smith; it was her gentle qualities and appearance that Tom had inherited. Apart from the large number of trophies that Tom had won – mainly in his amateur days, this tiny bedsit was very sparsely furnished. In one corner of the room was a small single divan bed: by its side, there was a straight backed wooden chair that Tom kept his pyjamas on, underneath were his slippers. Facing the bed, in the far corner, was a three-quarter size wardrobe, which had seen better days. Next to this, stood a small cupboard with two drawers: the top of this cupboard was littered with Tom's trophies – many of them looked as though they had seen better days. Some must have been fifty years old. Mick sat in an easy chair, alongside a drop-leaf table, while Tom prepared their coffee in a small recess, which served as a kitchen. The bedsit was clean and bright.

Mick sat and watched Tom's movements as he was preparing their nightcap. "If there is such a thing as God," thought Mick, "Then why does he allow someone as gentle as Tom to end his life in this lonely way". Mick and Danny had witnessed the deterioration of Tom's health over the past couple of years. As he watched his old friend perform the simple task of preparing a cup of coffee, he wondered how long it would be before Tom could not distinguish between making a cup of coffee, or a cup of tea.

"It was good to see you in such a talkative mood tonight Tom, you haven't gone and got yourself a little woman have you, and are keeping her to yourself?"

"Of course not, Mick. I'm off them for Lent".

"Away with you man, a little lady friend would do you the world of good".

Mick stretched his legs and slipped his hands into his trouser pockets. He pushed his head back onto the chair and looked into Tom's face, with a mischievous grin and waited for his reply.

"Me, have a woman. Do you remember the last one I had pushed onto me by Danny, with his good causes. Do you remember Mick? Yes, you remember alright, sitting there with a grin on your face."

Mick was pleased at the way Tom confronted him.

"The one with the monkey, remember? It was when I had

that tatty little flat – the one I had before I got this place. 'Tom', Danny said to me, 'Will you let this poor woman stay with you for a few days. She's stranded in Liverpool and has nowhere to go. If you take her in, I will try and get her fixed up with some accommodation'. Yes, that's Danny, the Good Samaritan".

Mick snorted with laughter. "It was alright for you and Danny, Mick. You did not have to live in the same house as the silly cow. I don't know who was the worst, her or the monkey. Not only did I have to take the woman in, I had to suffer her monkey as a lodger as well. Yes, you can sit there grinning like a cheshire cat but I was the one who had to suffer the silly woman for two weeks; that is until I rebelled".

Still with his legs stretched out in front of him with both hands in pockets, Mick concentrated on the movements and speech of Tom. He could see the smile building up on Tom's strong features. Although this woman had disturbed Tom's quiet existence, he could always see the funny side of his encounter with her.

"It's often said that animals grow to look like their masters", said Tom "But, I tell you Mick, that one was possessed by that monkey. She was a terrible sight when she went into a rage, walking around in her bare feet with her teeth in a glass on a chair by the side of her bed. The only time she wore her shoes was when she went out to buy food for herself and that monkey. I felt in mortal terror of the two of them. When the postman called it would be first to the door – moved like a blasted rocket".

"Who would be first to the door?" asked Mick.

"The monkey of course. You know quite well who I mean".

The look of delight left Tom's face for a brief moment because he felt that he had been rudely interrupted by Mick's nonsense.

"Where was I? Oh yes, the monkey. Well he would be at the door before I was out of my chair. It would be yelling with pleasure as it picked up from the floor what letters the postman had pushed through the letterbox".

"I wish I'd have had a monkey to collect my letters from the front door" said Mick.

"Will you stop interrupting me and let me get on with it. The next thing it would be sitting on my armchair, opening the mail, much the way you and I would open a letter, then it would proceed to read the damn thing".

"Now Tom, who is trying to make a monkey out of who" said Mick.

Tom was becoming annoyed at Mick's continued interruptions; the annoyance manifested itself by shakes of the head as Tom picked up his mug of coffee from the table as he was about to sit down. Mick could see that he had upset Tom by his frivolous behaviour.

"I'm sorry, Tom. It's just that I find the whole idea of the monkey opening your letters so funny. I know that you are not telling me a tall story, so please accept my apologies Tom, there was no harm meant".

"I know you meant no harm, Mick. Anyway, drink your coffee, it's lying there going cold".

For the first time, Mick saw the mug of coffee in front of him, realising then that he had become so immersed in Tom's description of the monkey that he had forgotten about it.

Sipping their nightcap, the two friends sat together in silence, apparently oblivious of each others presence. Mick broke the silence.

"Well, Tom, I will have to be leaving you. I've had a hard day today and I've got some heavy work ahead of me tomorrow".

Mick lifted himself from the comfortable armchair and stretched his arms above his head, but there was no response from Tom as Mick made ready to go. Tom sat with his coffee in his hand, and in silence gazed towards the floor.

"Tom, I will be off now".

There was no reply, apart from a nod of the head. As Mick opened the door to leave Tom alone in his little bedsit, Tom looked up from the floor.

"Oh, goodnight Mick, God Bless".

Mick closed the door behind him, not daring to tell Tom that Danny had passed away.

Prayers Before Work

They arrived at the construction site over-burdened with a carpenter's tool box in one hand a well used suitcase in the other. The bus journey from Reading Station to the site at Burfield was a miserable experience for them, made worse because they had no idea just what to expect. They had no written contract, just had to take the chance that the job would be there when they arrived on that cold February day in 1956, another concern was where they would sleep that night?

The conditions on this site, miles out into the countryside of Berkshire, were very primitive. Hundreds of men worked up to their knees in mud, without a canteen or any welfare facilities. Toilet facilities were so bad that it was more hygienic to take a shovel and find a quiet spot in a field. The management had no regard whatsoever for the lives of the men they employed. Every day, men would be sent inside concrete bunkers to strip away the steel plates which held the concrete in place.

The living conditions that most of the men were subjected to were appalling. Changing these conditions would have been difficult due to Trade Union officials being about as rare as caviar on a building site. The management had provided an ex-army camp a couple of miles down the road from the site. The beds turned out to be clean, but the food was lousy. Men on the Burfield site in Berkshire had come from almost every part of the British Isles. From as far as Ireland and Scotland and the North of England, they had travelled not because they were seeking adventure, or to look at what was on the other side of the hill, but because they had been driven there by economic factors beyond their control. The only comfort that most of them could look forward to was in the local pubs and bars around the area.

Gordon moved about the scaffold, fixing into place the form work made of heavy timber. He had left his wife and baby daughter in Newcastle so that he could find work, 1956 was not a prosperous year in Newcastle for construction workers, so Mick also went to find employment in the South.

Like the rest of the carpenters, Gordon would finish his section of form work each day, ready for the concrete to be poured in the next – and so it went on.

February is not the best time of the year to work on a large construction site. If he hoped to be able to feed his young family, Gordon's life in the coming months would consist of the daily monotony of struggling through mud and scrambling onto scaffolding.

Gordon stood about five feet eight inches. He had a strong, handsome face, which wore a dark complexion; his shoulders and legs were strong, his waist slim. Nature had been kind to Gordon and it had brought him to full maturity at the age of twenty-two. He was a quiet young man, who never swore, with the movements and disposition more suited to a man of the church.

At the end of each day, buses provided by the company would take the men back to the camp. Hundreds of them would live like animals, sleeping in long dormitories if you were a labourer; or in a room that held four men if you were a tradesman like Gordon. Married and single men lived like prisoners of war, company was to be found in the local pubs if you were lucky enough to get into one as they were generally overcrowded. There were times when prejudice was displayed by local landlords; if you had any accent other than a Southern one, you ran the risk of being asked to "drink up and get out", there was of course safety in numbers though.

Later, there would be the long walk back to the camp,

where, lying in your pit, you would think about your family back home. Eventually, exhaustion would overcome you. Every morning, Gordon would be out of bed an hour before his workmates. He would be first in the canteen, then he would wander off to the little Catholic church which lay down the road away from the camp. Always, though, he would be ready to board the bus at the appointed time for the ride back to the construction site.

Alongside the main gates of the site, the buses would pull into the compound. All the men would file through the gates to 'clock-on' at eight o'clock. Gordon was soon in position on the scaffolding, stripping out the timber form work from the concrete, which was hopefully set. Most of the men were engaged in the same operation, others would be in the fields digging trenches and laying pipes. About a hundred yards away from Gordon was another young carpenter working on his own section of the job. He was a fine big lad, not unlike Gordon in build. Standing about five feet eleven his hair was fair. Although strong, his face however did not portray the same strength of character as Gordon's.

This young man had left his home in Dublin, unlike most of his Irish comrades, he cared little for work. Frequently, he could be seen walking about his section of the job making a nuisance of himself. Gordon, because of his quiet manner, was easy prey for him.

"Hey, Geordie, have you been to church this morning? Suppose it helps to make you work better".

The taunts would go on until his voice would disappear into the next section, where he would make further trouble.

Sensible men hold their tongues on a construction site, except when they are seeking better pay and working conditions from the management, but the Dublin boy was fast becoming a pain in the neck. He was also a bully and he had found the church-going Catholic boy an easy target for his loose tongue.

Gordon spoke to few people on the site. Those men who were close to him knew that he only lived for his little family in

44

Newcastle, where he would rather have stayed.

I had been with one or two other Stewards trying to sort out some of the welfare facilities and was returning to the section I was working on at the site, when one of the men shouted to me.

"He's been at it again".

I was informed that Gordon had been suffering more abuse from his tormentor, and that things had come to a head.

"They're going to settle it once and for all", said some of the men.

How would Gordon fare, I wondered, in a physical encounter with this very strong Dublin boy? I feared for his safety as I imagined the outcome of the intended fight.

During the course of the day, the incident left my mind, due to the pressure of work, and the Trade Union problems on site.

At five o'clock that night, with the other men, I made my way through the slime and mud to the site office. I was called upon to put my card in the clocking machine. Placing my card in the machine it stamped my finishing time on it. Just beyond the site office and the high fence, lay the huge compound where the buses parked.

Before me, was a sea of men who had formed themselves into a huge circle. The scene reminded me of something I had read about the Yukon in the days of the Gold Rush, where men would stand in their hundreds watching two gladiators proving themselves to their eager awaiting audience that they were men. The reasons for the confrontation no longer mattered; all that mattered was that two men were defending their honour, standing bare-knuckled and toe to toe, unconsciously using the Queensbury Rules. Those of us in the audience who knew the two protagonists saw only two human beings doing battle with their fists. One no longer looked at the Dublin boy as a big mouthed bully, or at the Newcastle man as a quietly spoken good Catholic boy; we felt only admiration for the way the pair conducted themselves during that raw challenge.

The fight between the two men became faster; the punches were crisp and solid, but it was Gordon's punches that were landing on the target area with sickening precision. The Dublin boy's face started to resemble a battered tomato. As the battle continued, neither man showed signs of going down and the longer they fought, the greater my admiration grew. Their heads were used only for thinking with and their feet were used trying to avoid blows; their hands did the fighting.

Watching the battle unfold before me, I became uneasy and concerned. I realised that I was supposed to improve conditions for my fellow workers. Being a Shop Steward, I was supposed to settle any problems that the men had with the management; this was another problem. Slowly, I walked over to the two men, finding myself in the middle of the circle of men. Standing alongside the protagonists, I stopped the battle.

Some would say that the spectacle was raw, crude, uncivilised. Yet, those same people could admire the sharpness of the steel cutlass slicing a fellow human being in half and justify this action as being a necessary evil in times of war. Many would condemn this fight as an act of brutality, yet respect those with the viper's tongue destroying a man with character assassination to satisfy their own lust and greed for power. Nevertheless, the two men that I witnessed doing battle in a field were civilised enough to settle their differences over a pint of beer. What must be understood is that the working and living conditions created a breeding ground for those inadequacies prevalent in some men.

The following day, the young Dublin boy had to meet his girlfriend in London. She would encounter his badly bruised face and anguish would cover hers. Meanwhile, a smile would descend on the face of the management of the Burfield site, because they were the only winners in any confrontation which occurred between men whose only reason for being on sites like Burfield was to scratch a living out of the mud and slime.

Corduroy Pants and Khaki Shirts

It was a quiet Friday morning, Joey was making his way to the Pier Head for a cup of tea. The dock road was quiet, the traffic had not built up, the speedometer on his hackney cab showed twenty seven miles an hour, it gave him time to look about the Dock Road; "God, its changed", he thought to himself.

The early sunshine had pushed its way through the windscreen of the cab and on to Joey's weather-beaten face; he could feel the warmth of the sun descend deep into his body.

"It's good to be alive" he thought to himself.

Joey's mind kept drifting back;

"It's funny the way life goes, I can still remember walking along this road when I was just a kid and looking at all of the ships and imagining the romance of sailing away in them; God, I soon found out it was more hard work, and little romance", a smile came to his face; well, it wasn't a bad life, sailing the seven seas, and now its all gone; just empty docks and scrap yards, what a future to give our kids.

The sight of the Liver Birds in the distance snapped Joey from his thoughts, the cab radio was on low and giving out information, "I hope they don't want me to pick anybody up until I have had a cuppa tea".

The hackney cab swung its way to the right at the traffic lights past the Liver Buildings and on to the big plateau, in front of the large Pier Head buildings.

He was about to get out of his taxi when a grating voice came over his cab radio, "Anybody in town, or by the Pier Head?" came the crackling voice over the well-worn radio.

47

"Delta one calling, I'm at the Pier Head", said Joey.

"Go to Lime Street Station, pick up Mr. Brady" said the operator at the other end of the radio.

"Well there goes my cuppa, God knows when I will get one now", thought Joey.

Joey made his way to Liverpool's main line station; "I hope it's a good fare and not just going around the corner" he thought.

The cab pulled its way into the station. "Are you Mr. Brady?"

"Yes, we want to go to Esk Street Police Station" came a nervous reply.

Mr. Brady was holding a pretty little girl of about eighteen months and standing next to him was another little girl of about three years and a young woman, who looked small and frail, the strain of travelling showed in her movements as she entered the cab, Mr. Brady getting the children in first, then he gently put his hand on the young woman's shoulder, like a shepherd guiding his sheep into the security of his pen, as he helped her into the taxi cab.

Mr. Brady leaned forward, "Do you know Esk Street Police Station?" he said, with a Northern Irish accent.

Joey nodded his head.

"I was told that it was down by the docks".

"Yes, that's right," replied Joey. A half-smile came to Joey's face, when he felt the strange feeling in his stomach.

"Yes, I know Esk Street Police Station", he thought to himself.

"We have been travelling since early this morning, we set off from home in Ipswich at one o'clock last night", said Mr. Brady.

"I see" said Joey, looking at the young couple and the children through his rear view mirror. The young woman with her arms around the two children, her face said many things; she seemed as though she wanted to burst into tears, but he could see the restraint in her face, so as not to alarm the children. The young man wanted to talk and he could see that Joey was a good listener; Joey had that sort of face, although his passengers could ony see one side of it, as he half-turned his head to them.

The young man leaned forward in his seat, one hand holding the other, Joey could see him in the mirror, the young man's composure had gone.

"All our money is gone in paying our train fare, and the taxis as well. We had to borrow money off the neighbours, but the Police are paying our fare when we get to the boat", said Mr. Brady.

"Its my mother, she's been hurt and we don't know how she is" said Mrs Brady.

"You see it's my wife's Ma, they told us last night" said Mr. Brady. The pain they were suffering was flowing out of them.

"We don't know what it will be like when we get to Belfast" said the young wife, her arms pulling her children in closer to her.

Joey felt very uneasy listening to the young couple, he had no idea what they were talking about, but he felt for them. Joey had now forgotten if it was a good fare in the back of his cab. His only concern was for the young family in his charge, though it be only for a few minutes. The strange feeling came back in his stomach as he thought about Esk Street Police Station. Joey could not have been much older than the little three year old. His own family were in despair like so many of the people in his community who lived in the area surrounding Esk Street Police Station. Joey's mind was racing back like a salmon making his way back up a fast flowing river. The big heavy green door and the big brass tap in the Police Station yard. He could see his mother holding his hand while she stood in a queue of women and children in the police yard. It was warm inside the police station and the lights were bright, unlike the gas lamp in his home. Joey could see the folding tables in straight lines and well-dressed ladies standing at the other side of the tables. Lots of clothes in a big heap. Children sitting on the floor trying them on. Corduroy pants and khaki shirts to match the colour of the pants. Joey sat next to the rest of the kids waiting for his turn to receive police clothes from the benevolent fund.

"Have you got your ticket?" said one of the well-dressed ladies. His mother pushed the ticket forward on the table, the ladies of charity dished out their wares.

Joey looked back in his rear view mirror. Mr. Brady's voice catching Joey's attention again.

"The children have not eaten since last night. They have slept most of the journey", said Mrs. Brady, her eyes downcast, her arms still protecting her children as she held them close to her. The little family fell silent for the remainder of the journey.

The solid Yorkshire stone walls protected the police station, Joey walked into the station yard, its large green wooden door drawn back to the inside of the stone wall, the large brass tap still protruded from the wall.

Joey smiled as he thought about the times he and his brothers stood with buckets and bowls in their hands, along with dozens of other people waiting their turn to collect water from the big brass tap.

Joey could remember his mother turning the tap in the hovel where they lived and the water failing to appear. Joey never knew why the water dried up, but when it did, out would come buckets and off he would go to Esk Street Police Station.

Joey rubbed his hand over the grey Yorkshire stone of the building as he walked towards the main entrance. Mr Brady and his little family followed, tired and weary. Mr. Brady led the way up the three steps leading to the reception area, carrying what little possessions they had. Joey offered to help carry some of them, but Mr. Brady declined the offer. His frail wife walked in behind him, her two children by her side.

A Police Sergeant stood behind the mahogany topped desk, his two large hands laying flat on the polished wood. He was a big man with the round, weather-beaten face of a middle aged man, his face gave off a friendly smile that radiated from his blue eyes, his hair was wavy, but going grey.

The lights are still bright, thought Joey, although it was a fine summer day. The lack of windows necessitated them being on twenty-four hours.

"Are you Mr. Brady?" said the Sergeant before Joey could introduce the Brady family.

The Sergeant lifted the heavy flap of the desk and came around to the front.

"I suppose you're hungry" he said, looking at Mrs. Brady.

"Well, we will soon put a stop to that" he said, still taking an interest in the Brady family. The Sergeant offered his hand to the oldest child.

"I've got the kettle on" he continued.

Joey walked into the kitchen with the Bradys. A strong smell of bacon filled the air.

"Sit yourselves down, we will soon get things moving and it won't be long before we get you down to the boat".

Joey looked at the Sergeant, who had his back to him, preparing a breakfast for Mr. Brady and his family and towards Mrs. Brady, her two children clinging to each side of her, sitting on the wooden bench, beside the plastic top table. The scene before Joey filled him with emotions and memories, so intertwined that he was not sure whether he should shout for joy or burst out crying.

The Police Station was the last remnant of the community Joey had grown up in. The families he knew had been scattered to the winds. His emotions were coming from the pit of his stomach. He wanted to shake the hand of the Sergeant, who still had his back to him, but he knew that would make him look foolish, for how could the Sergeant and the Brady family possibly understand what he was feeling?

"I will have to go now Mr. Brady. I wish you well on your journey" said Joey glancing towards Mrs. Brady and her two children.

51

"Thanks Sarge" said Joey. He walked out of the kitchen and into the station yard, once again rubbing his hands over the Yorkshire stone.

Joey made his way to the Pier Head for the belated cup of tea. The radio was silent in his cab.

Joey was much calmer as he sat watching the children feeding the pigeons on the Pier Head's Plateau.

A sombre group 1934

A day in the life of Whacker

Whacker is a nice simple sort of man, who was quite sure that people would sit-up and take notice of him when he sent off a written profile of himself to a National Newspaper. He was only a building labourer, but was sure people would be interested in his working day.

"Every morning I get out of bed at 6.30 a.m. – Monday to Friday that is – but before I get out of bed, I usually have a little think about the building site that I work on, give myself a good scratch and then climb out of bed.

Always, I wash my hands before making my way downstairs, like a man in a drunken state; that is what comes of working on a building site; carrying and climbing all day, so that after a hard days work, you are so tired that it's still with you the next morning.

The kitchen is the next stop to put on the kettle, switch on the trannie and listen to Radio City. Breakfast is always the same, helping to keep my body in good shape for the building site – it would soon be noticed if there were signs of the flab. There I go, getting carried away, but I am always like this first thing in the morning. No matter what happens, I will always have that first mug of tea with one sugar.

I take a cup of tea up to the missus every morning and try not to wake the kids. Have you ever heard five kids squawking first thing in the morning. "Dad, can I have a cup of tea?" That's all you get out of them, and me trying to get ready for work.

At about 7.00 a.m., I make my way to the bus stop.

I get to the site at 7.55 a.m. At 8.00 a.m. I start work, carrying timber for the carpenters. "Come on", the General Foreman will say to me, "Get a move on whack". He usually calls me Whack, and so do the lads.

At 10.00 a.m. I have my tea-break. Lasting ten minutes, the tea-break gives me a chance to do my bet, which will be dropped into the betting shop at noon.

Most of my working day is spent carrying timber for the carpenters. "Come on Whack, hurry up, we're on bonus" cry the carpenters. The pace of this work is the reason I am like a drunk first thing in the morning. I suppose the construction industry sounds strange to those not familiar with it: it sort of grows on you. Starting at the age of fourteen years, you quickly learn to live with the biting wind and rain in the Winter. I could have chosen many other occupations, but I am sure that I would not have been happy if I had done – job satisfaction is very important. I did toy with the idea of going into medicine, or carving out a musical career for myself. However, I know my family feel I made the right choice. One of my sons will be following me into the construction industry, and the other boy will go into a Manpower Services Work Experience scheme. I hope it will give him a good start, having the chance to learn how to work.

By 6.00 p.m. I am home and the squawking kids will have had their evening meal. My evening meal is the one I enjoy most; it allows me to talk to the missus in peace, and I always give her a kiss on the cheek for having to look after the squawks all day.

After such a fulfilling day, I read the paper and fall asleep until about 9.00 p.m., then if I am in the mood, I will call into my local and have a game of darts and a couple of pints of Guinness.

You will always find me back at home for 11.00 p.m. I am one of those people who need plenty of sleep. If I don't get a good night's sleep, my brain is numbed the next morning. My colleagues would soon notice if I was not my usual chirpy self.

By 11.30 p.m. the tom cat will have been kicked out, and the missus and I will have retired to bed, with a cup of cocoa."

The Gift of Eloquence

We never planned to go to Ballydaly, three miles outside of
Millstreet in West Cork. It just came out of the blue, so to
speak. It was Janet our neighbour, she had booked this little
cottage in West Cork and was unable to take advantage of
spending two weeks in Ballydaly due to unforeseen family
matters. So here we are, Pauline, myself and the two kids,
making plans for our trip on the ferry Leinster, sailing from
Liverpool to Dublin.

We arrived in Dublin at 7.30 a.m. on the Saturday, ready for
our drive in my old car, a 1975 Triumph Toledo, in the hope
that it would make it to West Cork, without us having to push
it.

After many hours on the road we arrive. The bungalow
stood there facing us at the top end of a field. Entrance was
along a narrow path, just wide enough for a car or a tractor.
On sight of the bungalow, Katy said "That can't be it, its too
nice", but sure enough it was for us.

We were shown around the place by Mrs. O'Brien, the
owner. She was a pleasant lady with the sort of West Cork
accent that makes you feel at ease. Before leaving she told us to
give her a call any time if we were in need of anything, she
lived in a farmhouse at the back of our bungalow.

The children, Peter and Katy, soon made friends with two
little dogs that lived on the farm.

After a wash and a bite to eat, we all went into the town of
Millstreet, Pauline and the kids did some shopping and I had
a drop of Guinness. We did not stay too long as we were all

57

a little weary after the travelling, so back down the three mile road to Ballydaly and our little bungalow.

The next day, Sunday, we arose by 10.30 a.m. and by 11.30 a.m. we had finished our breakfast in our temporary home. Peter came into the kitchen with two pints of fresh milk, delivered by our landlady's 13 year old son.

Breakfast over, we set off for Millstreet. We arrived at midday. Just as you enter the town there is a library and car park on the left, and a general shop and garage on the right, with a number of farm machinery and tractors outside, in for repair.

We park the car and make our way onto the High Street, just in time to see the procession and the lone piper leading them. It was then I realized this was the feast of Corpus Christi, so we decided to join them to the church.

After we left the church, which had been packed to the doors, we did some shopping in the Supermarket in the high street. We then set off for our bungalow and some dinner.

At 3.00 p.m. we se out for Kilarney for a couple of hours. Peter was glued to the TV and so declined the chance of seeing more of West Cork, or Kerry, that afternoon.

Pauline, Katy and myself set off on the seventeen mile journey to Kilarney.

Everywhere we looked we saw beauty. Katy repeatedly pointed out everything of interest. On the hillsides just up from he road, we could see bungalows, being built or just finished. They were not clustered together, but dotted around the hillsides, just like the old cottages. We were so engrossed in what we saw on our journey, that Kilarney soon loomed up on the horizon.

We walked around the town as though we were on a reconnaissance mission, finding out about all the things we could do and see on our return later in the week.

The following day was a lazy one, so we decided to stay local and have a look at the scenery in the Ballydaly area.

We all had a stroll down to the stream just below our little house. The stream had a narrow road bridge running over it.

The very sight of this stream of clear water that comes down from the Derrnassaggart Mountains and separates our little piece of West Cork from County Kerry, was enough for the kids to climb down the bank, strip off their socks and shoes and wade into the water, also in pursuit were the two local dogs, who had adopted us during our stay in Ballydaly.

The following day we return to Kilarney, with a firm plan, drawn up by the kids. We have, or should I say they have, decided we hire a push-bike each. The hire charge was £2.50 per machine for 24 hours, not that we would be in the saddle for 24 hours.

Fitting ourselves out with bikes was a great idea, a large frame for myself, a lady's bike for Pauline. Katy decided on a gents bike. Now we come to Peter; he was still trying out every machine in the shop, but at last, and a little reluctantly he chose a smaller frame. So off we go, a little shaky at first, on the two and a half miles to the lakes of Kilarney.

If you want to see the lakes and you have the energy, I can assure you this is the way to do it. By the time we arrived at the lakes, Pauline and himself, not the kids, were a little saddle sore.

Just as well we hired the bikes, it makes it so much easier to navigate the nature trails around the lakes.

We came upon Muckross Abbey. Its ruin is still cared for, even though it was founded in 1448 by Donal McCarthy, Chieftain of Desmond, for the Observantine Franciscans. While walking over the Abbey your mind tries to wander back over time to the men who built this monument and cared for it for so long. The stonework for this building came out of the ground, was shaped and put together to form the structure and many like it, and remained part of the land from which it came. Stark contrast from modern man with his ability to process and destroy the natural beauty of stone, trees and the rest of nature, for the madness of the concrete and plastic jungles that most of us live in.

When you are in a place like the Kilarney Lakes and so close to nature, you don't always need a bike to get carried away.

Peter, on sight of the water, wanted to strip off and jump straight into the lake. He is an 11 year old who loves water and swimming. Wherever our travels take us, Peter would have his swimming trunks with him. Much to his disgust swimming was not allowed in the lakes, although we did manage to find a quiet spot to sit down and have a sly paddle in a shallow part of the lake.

Muckross House in the National Park was a sight to be seen. The gardens were a feast to anyone who loves nature.

The house is a good example of how the very wealthy lived, but that is not meant to degrade Muckross House. It was built in 1843 and is now administered by the National Parks and Monuments Service.

There are many examples of the trades carried out in the days of old, from Saddle Making to a Blacksmiths Shop. Many of the trades are still carried out, and you will see Craftsmen at work carrying on their craft.

Also in the house is a fine exhibition of local government in Kerry, during the 19th Century, together with different types of housing from 1812 to 1971. The local History Society have done a good job in presenting this exhibition.

By the time we rode back to Kilarney to return our bikes and pick up my old Toledo, we had had all we wanted from this very enjoyable day.

The following day, we hope to kiss the Blarney Stone, so off we go on our journey from Ballydaly up to Millstreet, then out on the open road to Macroom, then continue to Coachford, and the last lap, Blarney Castle.

The beauty that unfolded before us made my eyes moist as I drank in the power and strength of this wonderful land.

The month of June and West Cork go well together. Most of the trees and fields are in full bloom. The little showers of rain we would run into seemed to have a smile on their faces, as though mother nature was playing games on us.

The little villages we passed through had a magic of their

own. Places like Carriganinny, Dripsey and Inishcacarra, one's imagination can easily be taken over. If Judy Garland was to step out onto the road with her little animals and strange characters from the film "The Wizard of Oz", I doubt if I would have been surprised.

The new bungalows and old cottages that were stepped up from the road blended so much into the background that they looked for all the world like large plants with many different colours.

The road to Coachford was so natural with its twisting and dipping and turning every hundred yards and with all the wonder of nature to be seen everywhere, so unlike the flat, monotonous and drab roads that run through cities.

Without any warning from the right of the road and spread out before us was the River Lee, that comes down from the Shehy Mountains. The road followed the twists and turns of the river for many miles. If there is such a thing as paradise, then I am sure this journey is part of it. The river was so wide in parts that we first thought it was a series of lakes.

We stopped a couple of times to inhale the soft breeze and fresh air. The narrow bank that ran from the roadside where we stood, was covered in a pale green grass that gently made its way down to the water's edge. This was a section of the river that was wide and looked more like a lake. On the opposite shore, rising from the water, were many fields covered with trees and vegetation in many shades of green.

Each time we stopped we had trouble in restraining Peter from stripping off and plunging in the river. I hope his extravagance for ploughing into water will not extend to a liking for Guinness when he is older.

Eventually we arrived at Blarney Castle. The sight of the castle had the kids excited, also Pauline and I. After paying our entrance fee we found ourselves in the grounds of the castle. It was tempting not to go into the fairy glade first, so up we go, climbing the 100 stone steps. It can be reached by any age group, young or old, by taking your time. The younger ones being a little bit more adventurous in their haste to reach the top.

We reached the top and there it was, the Blarney Stone, the fairy tale come true. No longer did we have to think about it, or wonder if this object had come from the fertile mind of some Irish story teller in days gone by.

There, ready to be kissed by all those who had the nerve to lay on their backs looking for all the world as though they were waiting for "Madam Guillotine", to drop on them. The head goes down, the face pushed forward, ready to kiss that Emerald of the Emerald Isles, the Blarney Stone.

Those of us who did have the nerve to kiss the Blarney Stone have now been sent forth with the "Gift of Eloquence", which the stone bestows. Well that's what the legend says and I am of the opinion that it is true?

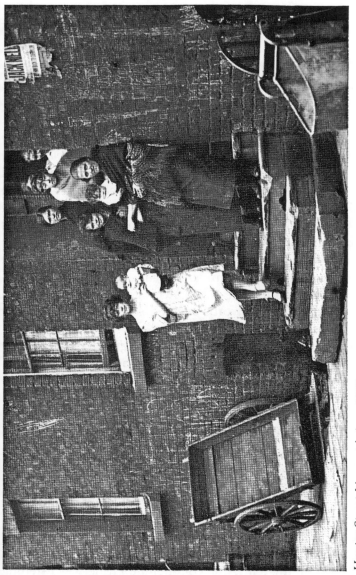

Hunter Street Liverpool circa. 1927

The Student

She sat cradling her text books like a mother holding her baby close to her breast while she gently patted its back. Jackie looked more like a girl of sixteen than the nineteen year old English Literature student who has wandered into the sitting room of the old Victorian house, where she had a bedsit; the room was occupied by two other students. Her movements took up a rocking motion as she pulled the books closer to her whilst she watched the television. She did not appear to notice any other person in the room, as she gave a running commentary on the programme she was watching. No-one in the room interrupted her, for her words seemed so personal; not really meant for the ears of others.

"I don't suppose they will show Fermanagh; it's a lovely County. But of course I'm bound to say that", said Jackie.

"Enniskillin – it would be nice to see on the television", Jackie's eyes were fixed on the black and white screen.

Far nicer if it was in colour she thought to herself.

The camera picked up a small boat, a gentle breeze was lifting the bow of the small craft, but not enough to disturb the man who was the sole occupant of the tiny craft.

"The waters are blue, you know".

Nobody answered in case they altered the flow of Jackie's observations.

"Well, it could be the blue waters of Lough Erne".

The room was silent except for her speaking; the only other sound was from the television commentator. She was listening

64

to him describing a world she knew – although she had not explored so much of the North.

"The divisions – the divided people – my people they are talking about".

Her thoughts still flowed for all to hear and the man in the small craft kept on fishing in the gentle breeze on the peaceful lough.

Opening wide, Jackie's eyes tried to hold back the tears.

"Have you ever been to Fermanagh; it is a lovely part of the world?"

The text books were clutched tighter, whilst Jackie's feelings and recollections came flowing out.

"It doesn't have to be like that; my country and our people divided, my family work hard, my father died too young, working the land to feed us".

The fisherman in his boat returned to the screen.

"My father used to fish in the lough. He was a good man, never hurt anyone".

Everyone just sat and listened, not daring to utter a word, a little sniff and a ray of light shot across Jackie's eyes.

"It's good to see a programme about Ireland, showing us as a people who have a love of nature. We are part of that nature; we have lived and worked the land for thousands of years. Our entire culture evolved from the land; our legends, our mythology were given meaning from the land".

Jackie paused, as though waiting for a response from the rest of us, sitting silent in the room and not wanting to disrupt her stream of thought.

"We are good people. Nice to see the countryside instead of the tragedies of urban city life. With a little luck, we may see the village I come from, Tempo. Yes, and Enniskillin – a lovely little town".

The images came to the screen and Jackie saw the lough and green villages back down the passage of time to her childhood; a childhood knowing no peace; walking past men with strange uniforms, driving ugly vehicles, as though they were in a sinister part of a lovely landscape.

The man in the boat appeared once again onto the screen.

"It could be lower Lough Erne", said Jackie with a gentle rocking motion from her body, with her text books still clutched to her bosom, her eyes and mind still held by the mirror that was a television screen, producing the images she longed to see.

The pain of the last few months came to the surface of her being, like it had been exorcised from her; memories of an evil landlady being spirited away, as she watched her lovely Fermanagh. Jackie let go of the bad experiences of her former landlady; a woman who had given the second year student a hard time in her first taste of private accommodation since she had left Fermanagh. Jackie's student friend had tried to protect her from the cruel remarks made by the landlady with the viper's tongue.

"Go back to Ireland, you Irish bastard. You're all the same", she would scream each time the television newsreader gave a bad press about Ireland.

She would bang on the door, "You're all the same", screeching at the five foot nothing Jackie through the thin panels of the door.

The commentary from the documentary kept Jackie's attention – a copy of Seamus Heaney's 'North' lying on top of the rest of the text books.

"I wonder what she would say if she was watching this programme?" said Jackie.

Her gaze moved from the television screen and she smiled.

"I bet the old witch would still have some adverse comment to make."

Jackie's fellow lodgers smiled back, but made no comment; it was unlike Jackie to make snide remarks, even about people as vile as her previous landlady.

"Yes, that's my homeland; it's lovely isn't it?"

Her face had become radiant. The rocking motion had stopped, her back straightened; her whole being seemed free from the months of torment. She knew that she was among friends at last; friends with whom she could express her innermost feelings.

The room became silent, as the programme came to an end, and Jackie recalled a fragment of a poem;
This refuge offers continuity;
A growing where you will know
The changing of season.
Jackie stood up, still clutching the books. She smiled at her friends with a mixture of embarrassment and satisfaction and then left the room.

Leo

When I first met him I never thought for one minute, that one day I would buy his house. Leo Farrel was my neighbour and getting on in years, he was turned eighty years old. He was a big man, over six foot tall with a good head of hair. He also had a very good dress sense, and he was conservative in his appearance. He hailed from County Cork but I never found out exactly what part he was from, he could even have been from the same area as my own family, but somehow we never seemed to get round to discussing it.

Leo was a popular man amongst his neighbours, he could be described as a gentleman in both appearance and manner, a man who bothered few people. Well meaning people suggesting the Social Services or a home help in order to help him would be met by look of disdain and a positive shake of the head.

I know of only one other person who was allowed to get close to him and that was his next door neighbour. She saw to it that he had a good Sunday dinner every week. He would spend a couple of hours talking to her husband, an ex-ship's master. They had plenty in common, Leo being a ship's radio officer all of his working days. Even when his days at sea finished he still continued to work for Marconi Marine.

The large photograph of Leo at a company reunion dinner still takes pride of place in my home. The home that was once Leo's. The photograph was taken in 1946, depicting many Marconi people, sitting at the tables, Leo was sitting at the table nearest the camera.

The house is a large Victorian terrace house, with six steps leading up to the front door, it even has the original bell-pull. You know, the type that had a row of bells hanging from a wall in the kitchen, so that the servants could answer the door for their employer.

Inside the house could be found many effects belonging to Leo. Items that he had discarded, such as the large photographs of his working colleagues.

Whenever you set foot in the house it seemed to have the stamp of Leo on it. It was as though he was letting you know that he had been around and he was leaving his mark on life, like the young man carving his name on the bark of the tree.

None of the rooms had electrical sockets that could accommodate items such as the electric kettle or radio, but nevertheless you could see Leo's electrical genius come into good use, from the light sockets he would boil his kettle and his radio could also be plugged into the same adaptor.

In the basement of the house could be found many parts of Marconi type old radios and all the bits and pieces that are part of a radio network. Not being a man that was tuned in to that sort of thing, it was very much a foreign language to me.

One of the many things that Leo left in the house was an old microphone. Leo told his friends that it was used by King George V, when he came to the City of Liverpool and declared the New Mersey Tunnel linking Birkenhead with Liverpool was open. Leo had the job of installing the public address system that day in 1934, so it was his proud boast that the public address system he had in his possession was the very mouthpiece the King spoke into on that momentous occasion.

Perhaps Leo's brush with Royalty is tied up with his own ancestry, perhaps a 'High King of Ireland' (Ard-Ri) for it was in his early days as a sea-going wireless operator that he was given the post of Number One Wireless Operator on the Royal Yacht, but alas, it was not to be for he went down with appendicitis the very day he was supposed to join the yacht. The Royal Yacht was not the only ship on the sea, and the sea was good to Leo where ahead lay many adventures, this can be borne out by the hundreds of postcards from all over the world from the many friends he had made over the years.

Everything Leo possessed had to be in its proper place. Every postcard or letter he received would have written on it the date he received it. Leo left so many things in this house, the house I was so lucky to buy. He left like a man walking out into the darkness, shedding his clothes, not wanting to look back.

In a way Leo's possessions were his family, all of the things would remind him of the sea and his days with Marconi. It was good to be of some use to society, to have a skill that kept him in demand. Leo had never married, no sons, daughters or loving wife to greet each time he landed on the shores of Liverpool, but he had many friends of both sexes and he still kept in contact with Ireland. Many of the postcards he received bore witness to that. Even the Cork Examiner was sent to him from Ireland, enabling him to keep in contact with County Cork, despite the many years away from the place of his birth.

Leo said little about his birthplace, we all knew it was Cork, although just what part we never knew. Leo was an orphan and that was as much as we could find out about this very private man.

It is many years since he departed this world, although his presence still seems to remain in the house so many years later. The lagre photograph taken with his working colleagues still hangs on the wall and other discarded items still seem to cling to the place.

After the sale of the house was completed, Leo was invited to stay on, certain refinements were added to the place, like running hot water. The only hot water he had came from a gas geyser in the kitchen, but the lead pipes were so silted up, very little water passed through them and with the low pressure from the pipes, the gas geyser refused to work.

Electric socket points were also added to give further comfort and all the things that younger people take for granted, but were a luxury for Leo.

The day before the legal requirements for the sale of the house were complete, Leo was taken into hospital. In the meantime the house was busy, having a new face lift and the parts that Leo occupied got priority treatment.

Word coming back from the hospital was Leo was doing fine and would be home soon, but things changed. Leo seemed to convey to those who visited him that he had had all he wanted from life. It had nothing else to offer him.

Leo, being the gentleman he was, tried not to convey his feelings to his friends and just went to sleep.

Off to the washhouse

Mary Ann

Mary Ann looked across the table at Barney, filling his pipe with Erinmore tobacco, she could see the strength in his hands, he held the pipe with his left hand, his right packing the tobacco in tight.

He ripped a piece of paper from the old newspaper that was covering the table as a make-do tablecloth, he was careful not to upset the contents on the table. He screwed the strip of paper up and leaned forward to light it from the open fire in the grate.

Barney could see the reflection of the back of his hand in the shining oven door, the oven was part of the fire range, he could see the cavity at the side of the oven which allowed the heat from the open fire to warm the underside of the oven for cooking purposes.

Barney smiled as he straightened himself in his chair with the lighted paper that was drawn to his waiting pipe, after sucking the air into the pipe a couple of times the tobacco gave way to the pressure and ignited.

Mary Ann was sitting in her old windsor chair, her elbows on the arm rests. She kept looking at the strong hands that held the pipe, she wondered how he was going to cope with forced retirement from the sea.

Barney was all of five feet five inches in his stocking feet and he still retained a straight back and a firm body for an old sea dog, a term he would use when explaining what he did to feed himself and his family, his hair was still fair with just a touch of grey.

Mary Ann was proud that Barney's friends and family all regarded him as a smart and clean man with a good nature. He had given Mary Ann three handsome sons and three fine daughters; not that he had seen much of them. His life was the sea, and now it had been taken away from him because of old age.

His life was always influenced by the sea, he was born in Passage West, Cobb in County Cork. His father had been a Marine Engineer who worked at the Verloume Shipyard, but he was now a redundant sea dog cast up on the banks of the River Mersey.

Mary Ann sat in silence, her eyes down-cast looking at the white apron that covered her black skirt, the hem of which covered her ankles, but she could still see Barney as he leaned forward holding his pipe with his left hand whilst he lifted a large piece of coal to throw on the open fire.

The fire in the grate was ablaze. It gave the room a warm friendly glow in its quest to out-do the dim gas mantle that looked very frail in the holder hanging from the ceiling.

Two large pieces of coal, the tops of which were still black were starting to split from the heat and little blue flames of gas kept jumping up and down, capturing Barney's attention.

Several large gilt-framed photographs hung from the walls of the small, square room depicting the sons and daughters of Barney and Mary Ann. The faces in the large photographs seemed to take on a life of their own, each time the reflection from the fire flickered across the glass in the frames.

Barney sat back in his old wooden chair, his left hand holding the pipe in his mouth, his right hand cupping his elbow to give support to it. His blue eyes were on Mary Ann over the rim of his pipe that gushed forth a steady pall of smoke.

Barney saw that she was no longer the straight limbed, dark haired girl that had given birth to his children, she had aged much too soon. Barney felt a mixture of remorse and guilt.

"Six months I have been home with her", he thought to himself.

Six months out of forty-four years. Most of the time it would be a couple of weeks, then back to sea on the coffee run around the South American Coast, or the River Plate.

Mary Ann and Barney continued to sit in silence, each of them enjoying the warmth of the fire. Barney's eyes were still on Mary Ann. Barney thanked God that she was with him to look after him in his old age, he felt secure, like a baby in its mother's womb.

Mary Ann felt nervous, her eyes downcast, but she could see Barney smoking his pipe. It was strange to see him contented in his chair.

"At last I have him to myself", she thought.

She felt as though time was standing still, though time was passing them by. The kids had gone, but Polly the parrot was still in her green cage in the corner of the room.

Mary Ann could remember the times Barney would make plans to go home to Cobh, when the kids had grown up. Mary Ann shifted her gaze, Barney's hand seemed to tighten around the pipe, a short pall of smoke took a horizontal course towards the open fire, his hand lost its grip on the falling pipe, his eyes closed and his head fell forward. Mary Ann fell to her knees, her hands held Barney's face. She pushed her head to his chest, Mary Ann's body went limp, the tears flowed down her face as she looked into Barney's face.

Polly the parrot started to get excited, calling Barney's name. Mary Ann turned her head from Barney's chest, the tears still running down her cheeks. She looked towards Polly in her cage, the bird looked at Mary Ann, its wings flapping up and down, the way it would when it was too warm, in an effort to try and cool itself, or when she wanted to leave the cage to fly around the small square room, before it would perch on the mantlepiece above the fire.

Mary Ann still on her knees in front of Barney's limp body, wiping the tears from her eyes, reached out her right hand and rested it on the side of Barney's face.

"We will not be going home now my love, you have gone

away and left me again, just when I thought I had you to myself".

The bird started to flap her wings again. She was becoming agitated and calling out Barney's name.

"For God's sake be quiet will ya. You always knew when he was due home, you would jump up and down and now, damn ya, you know he's gone".

Mary Ann stood up and turned to the cage, leaned over it and pulled the folded blanket that lay at the back of the square cage over Polly.

Mary Ann turned to face Barney's sagging body in the chair. She put her right hand at Barney's back and her left hand under his knees and pulled his body onto the floor. She then spread an old blanket on the floor next to the body and rolled it over onto it, straightening his legs and arms.

She then brought a large bowl of water from the kitchen and placed it next to Barney's body. She stripped the clothes from the body, folding them in a neat pile on the table.

Mary Ann set about washing the body, kneeling on the blanket.

Mary Ann's mind was spinning as she continued to wash the prostrate body. "How many times have I washed my babies like this?" she thought.

Mary Ann finished washing the body and covered it with the remains of the blanket. She then pulled herself up onto her windsor chair to gain her strength.

"There's work to be done", she thought.

The Stowaways

"Who's goin'?"

All the hands went up, representing five grubby thirteen and fourteen year olds. Yes, they were all getting out, away from the bombed houses and the buildings that had been smashed by German bombs.

They knew that if they stowed away on one of the big ships that sailed down the River Mersey their lives would be full of adventure, they knew it to be true for had they not heard it from the older boys and men who lived in their street in Kirkdale. Lots of boys in Liverpool had stowed away and when the captain found them the ship would be well out to sea and he would sign them on as a member of the crew, so that was the way it would be.

"The only thing we need now is a ship", said Hogger Smith.

Hogger was the leader of the gang, he was fourteen and a half and worked on the docks as a can-lad. It was not every lad that could make a good brew of tea and if you made a good brew, the men would appreciate it and they would make his life that much easier.

Andy Doyle was number two, by virtue of the fact that his Dad was still at sea and he was a ship's Bosun, some of the lads said that means he is a Petty Officer, so Andy knew more about ships than the rest of them.

Joey Collins was number three, two of his brothers were seamen, but they were only able-seamen, not like Andy's dad who was a Bosun.

Mickey Mullens was next in line. Now Mickey was a good thief and had never been caught stealing from the bombed buildings, so he would know how to find food for them if needs be.

Then there was the quiet member of the gang, Sonny Nelson. He was cunning and smart and would always have any problems worked out while the rest of them were still counting on their fingers.

"It's not the ship we should be worrying about at this stage", said Sonny Nelson.

"It's getting past the copper on the dock gate".

"No problem", said Hogger, "I know where there's a loose board in the fence".

"When are we goin'" said Mickey Mullens.

"What d'yer say we go tomorra' night?" said Hogger.

Not a word was spoken, they stood silent.

"Right" said Hogger.

"See ya' all at the top of Haddick Street at seven o'clock tomorra' night."

The appointed hour came the following night and they were all prepared, but not a penny in their pockets. Not that many of them had pockets in their trousers. Three of them had pumps on; one had boots and the fifth had shoes, that was Andy Doyle. No overcoats to protect them from the cold winter nights and no hats to stop the rain from beating them on the head.

Hogger, the can-lad, surveyed his band of pirates. They were all ready for the great adventure that lay ahead. This was one expedition that did not believe in wasting time in preparing itself. From inception, right up to the hour that their plans would be put into operation only took twenty-four hours, no-one could deny them being men of action, even though they were only thirteen or fourteen years old.

In 1939, the year the second world war started, their only playground would be the air raid shelters in the streets of Liverpool, empty houses that stood like humans without flesh, skeletons that had once been homes filled with laughter and tragedy were now screaming for comfort and affection; just like the little men of action. The would-be adventurers would oblige by climbing all over the bombed houses and filling the empty spaces, if only for a few minutes. Then they would descend before one of the large bones of the skeleton fell and crushed the life out of them.

Hogger and his little gang had lived with the violence that fell from the sky, but now the war was almost over and their education was complete.

Walking through the dock estate in the darkness of the cold November night, with piercing eyes searching for the ship of their dreams, Hogger and his gang walked, like five little characters in a tragic play, floating across the stage. There was silence broken only by Joey Collin's squeaking boots.

All the lights on the dock estate had been removed because of the war, but that would not deter the men of action. They had walked around for some hours during the early evening, in search of the right ship. Any old ship that lay tied up, still discharging its cargo would not be considered. The intelligence work was provided by Hogger and Andy Doyle, for were they not steeped in the knowledge of ships?

The five adventurers walked in silence, except for Joey's squeaking boots, towards the bridge which would take them to the west side of the docks. Then, they heard voices coming out of the inky darkness, from the direction of the bridge and a light lit up the doorway of the dock gateman's hut, on the far side of the bridge. The voices and the light from the door were soon gone and the men of action were cast into the darkness and silence once again.

"Can't go over the bridge now", said Hogger.

"If they come out of the hut we have had it".

"No need to worry", said Sonny Nelson, who was one step ahead of his little friends. "I've found a pontoon, and if we get a few pieces of wood we can row across like we do on the canal, when we sail on our raft".

That sailing experience on the canal came in handy, as they climbed down the ladder that was secured to the dock wall by a rope. With their piece of wood at the ready, to act as an oar, they set off into the darkness to get to the other side of the dock in their flat-bottomed pontoon, that was used for cleaning the side of the ships when they were in port. This was no pleasure craft. It was coated in oil and grease, but who was worrying about a little discomfort when you are on a great adventure.

The night was dark, except for the distant stars. The moon was also in the dark sky, but could not been seen with the naked eye.

The docks were without lights, to keep the enemy at bay, but the adventurers were pleased by the inky darkness.

Sonny Nelson's mind started to run away with him.

"If only we were commandoes just think what we could do with the enemy. We could sail across the sea and surprise them. Then we could shoot them in their sleep and we could sail away into the darkness and the next morning, when it was light, a big ship would see us and the captain would be so pleased with what we had done he would sign us all on, then we would be part of the crew".

"Come on Nello" said Hogger to Sonny Nelson.

He always called him Nello when he was annoyed with him.

"You're standing like someone in a trance. Pick that piece of wood up and start to row".

Hogger gave the orders and stood like the boy on the burning deck, except this was a greasy deck. Every time Joey moved on the moving deck of the pontoon his boots would squeak because he would be pulling them one way and the paint and grease the other way.

"Keep them boots quiet" said Andy Doyle, who was Hogger's number one, just like the first mate on a big ship. Hogger was the captain and Andy the First Officer.

The makeshift oars were slapping against the stinking water

of the dock and the pontoon was making for the far side. Its crew fell into silence with the fear of the unknown. Every time they moved their feet the filth from the dock would be lifted. Fear started to grip the adventurers. It seemed like an eternity before the pontoon hit the wall of the dock.

Hogger marshalled his ragged, cold and hungry troops.

"We will have to get some food" said Sonny Nelson.

"Let's look for a canteen" said Mickey Mullens.

"But they're all closed" said Joey.

"Of course they're all closed, so we will have to break in" said Mickey.

Mickey wanted to break into the storeroom, but his little gang would not want that, breaking the window to get in was the only damage they wanted to do, so dry toast it had to be, leaving the boys cold and hungry and hiding from footsteps in the dark, in case it was a policeman.

Sonny Nelson had been given the task of finding the right ship. It must be one making ready for sea.

"That looks like the right one" said Sonny.

"It's a big ship" said Mickey.

"It's taking on cargo" said Hogger.

"Yes, and I can see a guard at the top of the gangway" said Andy.

"We can't go on board until the guard goes away" said Joey.

His boots still squeaked each time he moved.

"If you don't stop them boots from squeaking, everybody on the ship will hear us" said Hogger.

Sonny Nelson went on another scouting mission, getting closer to the ship and watched the guard leave his post at the top of the gangway.

"Come on lads, he's gone" said Sonny to the little men of action.

They all jumped down from the bales of cotton that they had been laying on in the dock shed.

Tired and hungry, Hogger gave his orders. "Come on lads,

let's get on board before the guard comes back".

Once on board they found a lifeboat with a canvas cover.

"This will do us" said Hogger.

Hours went by and the dawn broke through with the sounds of footsteps, laughter and men talking.

"Wish I had a cigarette" said Mickey.

"Have a look out, see who's there" said Joey.

"It's soldiers" said Mickey.

"Hundreds of them".

"It must be a troop ship" said Hogger. Him being a leader and a man with special knowledge, being a can-lad on the docks.

"I'm going to ask them soldiers for a fag" said Andy.

"Yer can't" said Sonny Nelson.

"They will tell the Captain".

"No they won't" said Hogger.

"I need a fag".

"Aye, la, got a fag?" said Andy, pulling the canvas back to expose his comrades.

"What did I tell yer" said Hogger.

Sitting in a cloud of smoke under the canvas.

"They never told the Captain".

The cold and hunger was taking its toll on the men of action, when the canvas was pulled back by the Captain exposing Hogger and his little band of would-be adventurers who had just spent a cold night in a lifeboat on board a ship due to sail within the next week or 10 days.

The Aqutania alongside Princes dock circa. 1920

The Watchman

His duties consisted of walking up and down on the ship's deck, but never going out of sight of the gangway; the night watchman with his head pitched downward and the slow movements of his legs portraying a sad figure with a dark overcoat covering down to his ankles, and hanging insecurely from frail shoulders. The slow movement of his body as he walked the ship's deck, could have disengaged the heavy coat from his shoulders leaving it like an empty sack lying at his feet and exposing his frail body to the wind.

Jimmy at the age of fifty-two, was a physical wreck. His stomach had been cut away by the surgeon's knife, his sea days were over and this is how he would spend what little time he had left on this earth; not much of a reward for a lifetimes hard and bitter work at sea.

When Jimmy was twelve years old, St. Alexander's School Bootle would not be allowed to teach him any more, although he was a good and intelligent pupil, the best copper plate writer in the school, poverty and low wages coming into his family home, together with his romantic ideas of seafaring, would drive him away from school and set him upon the course that fate had, in her wisdom, or caprice, determined he should follow when he joined the Merchant Service.

Jimmy would have to wait until he was eighteen; a further four years, before he could join a ship. Many casual jobs on the docks would come first and his first job was with a firm of Ship's Engineers — working with the Boiler Makers — fetching and carrying for them and learning the most important art of how to make a good brew of tea.

Jimmy's young muscles started to develop, his shoulders grew stronger with the passing months. By the time he was sixteen he was no longer five foot four but had grown to five feet seven and his arms and shoulders had developed further, his blond hair cut short as was the custom of the time with the lads and men he worked with.

Jimmy's romantic feelings for the sea did not diminish during the next two years, the sea was all about him. Every day as he walked onto the dock estate he would see ships of all nations entering and leaving the port, ships tied up at the quayside loading or unloading their cargoes for foreign lands, countries, that some day he would visit.

Jimmy would look in envy at the young seamen who would pass him walking along the quays after embarking from a newly arrived ship. 'One day that will be me paying off from a ship with plenty of money in my pocket'. Jimmy's young mind would be full of adventures thinking of the day that would come when he would be 'somebody' in the street where he lived.

Time passes very slowly when you are sixteen waiting to be eighteen, and he could hardly contain himself awaiting the wonderful day when he would be able to go to the shipping office and 'sign on' for his first ship; and sample the great adventures that surely lay ahead. In the meantime however he was to toil during the long summer days and dreary dark hours of winter with the ship repair gangs. Sometimes being laid off from work for a couple of weeks at a time because the work was only casual.

His body was getting stronger and he had grown to five feet ten. Despite some of the older hands in the gang that he worked with who tried to persuade Jimmy not to make his life the sea he never wavered for an instant, so taken up with his dreams was he.

'It's all work and no pay, and the food is lousy. It's no life if you get married'.

Jimmy had listened to all of the reasons as to why he should not go away to sea, but the time had come, he was getting out. It was time to make contact with the right people for the advice he needed. Jimmy's father was a seaman; not that he had seen much of him as he was always at sea or stranded in some South American port after missing his ship through drink. This meant his mother having her allowance stopped, (an allowance was a portion of a seaman's pay that was handed to his named next of kin ashore by the Shipping Company) in Jimmy's case it would be his mother. When an allowance stopped for any reason then the person named had the big problem of finding the money to replace it to possibly feed the family.

So this was the background which helped shape Jimmy's future plans. He made his way to the Shipping Office that his father and elder brother sailed for.

'So you want to go away to sea and be a stoker' the Shipping Master with little reading glasses perched on the end of his nose looked up at Jimmy with a look of amusement, Jimmy wondering to himself if he was about to be rejected.

'Well you will have to do the dirty work if you want to be a stoker' said the man still looking up at Jimmy, 'and you will have to be a hard man', he continued.

'How old are ye, eighteen?' the Shipping Master looked straight into Jimmy's eyes. 'Hard men you know, you will be sailing with very tough hard men, well if it's the sea you want, we will see what we can do for you. Okay, we will let you know'.

So off he went with a smile and joyous heart to await his call to the sea.

He was eighteen years old when he joined his first ship in Huskisson Dock, Liverpool, on a cold November day in 1918, just after the First World War had ended.

A ship that was to take him away from a 'land fit for heroes'. The only thing Jimmy had known during his young days in Liverpool was misery and poverty, so off he went to sea, this fine, good looking, budding sailor, with fair hair and blue eyes, slim frame and strong shoulders.

The second generation of an ex patriot Scottish father and Irish mother, he would sail from the port of Liverpool to distant and (to him at that time) enchanted lands far away.

The only romance however Jimmy McIntyre would get from his sea voyages would be the little time spent alongside the docks in foreign lands. Most of the time at sea would be a living hell for Jimmy and his shipmates below in the stoke hole; but, there were some 'good times' ashore with the lads, doing the sorts of things you could never tell your family about.

The steam ships that ploughed around the world's oceans were hungry beasts made of steel, their bellies had to be fed with coal twenty four hours a day, by young men that also had to be made of iron to match their charges.

Over the years Jimmy McIntyre was to sail in many ships even in a couple of Yankee boats mostly on the Coffee Run to South America. Jimmy's first few trips down below in the boiler room in front of the furnace was working as a trimmer pushing the coal forward for the experienced stoker the who would knock up the latch on the furnace door with his shovel, then lift a shovel full of coal and swing it round to face the furnace and throw the coal about ten feet off the shovel into the boiler, an action, which took a lot of strength and skill even from an experienced man.

Naval captains could majestically sail the seven seas, yachtsmen could fight nature, and each perhaps would get a little closer to God, but the ship's stoker would always be closer to the devil. You could always recognise a ship's stoker because even years after his sea days were over, his leather belt would be fastened at the back, an old custom from days gone by to stop the buckle from getting too hot from the open furnace and also to stop it digging into his stomach every time he bent to pick up a shovel of coal to pitch into the mouth of the monster.

Sailing ships and yachts had sails to catch the wind to move them across the oceans, and, they were only a fraction of the size of a steamer. The steam ship had young men of iron buried deep within its bowels shovelling continuously feeding its belly with coal, which in turn made the steam to move the giant pistons that would drive the ship's engines and make the propeller turn, moving the steamer across the seas.

All the energy that was needed to move those massive steam ships through fair seas and gale force winds, depended entirely by young men such as Jimmy McIntyre, because if left unfed, the monster furnace would stand there cold and empty, the pistons motionless, the engines useless, the screw gathering barnacles.

The inevitable fate of most of Jimmy's shipmates would be death before the age of sixty, the constant heat shrivelling the fluid from their bodies each time they went on watch. Four hours was a long time to spend in the boiler room of a steamer with the sweat running down your body and, to attempt to compensate, many pints of none too clean water would have to be consumed. The watch over they then climbed out of the stoke hold onto the open deck, sometimes to be greeted by the rays of the sun and a soft breeze and, at other times, by the chilling gale-force winds that would tear into a body covered in sweat, the walk along an uneven deck to the fo'csle head to rest in primitive conditions only added to the misery.

It was almost miraculous that any man would continue to subject himself to such a life, but, Jimmy's ship mates were modest men who would praise the ship that could get a good head of steam, a ship that would not demand too much from the energy in their solid muscles. Day and night the ship's engines would need attention, keeping them in good condition. Every year or two the ship would go into dry dock for a clean up and general inspection to make sure she was in a good order.

The stoker also would be given a brief periodic inspection by a none too concerned doctor to see if his heart was still in moderate working order and the strength was still there to allow him to carry out the function required, if not, then he too would be cast to one side like an old sack.

Stokers wore heavy boots to protect their feet from the hot steel plates that he stood on and this helped to keep his balance when he pitched the coal into the furnace. This was the life Jimmy McIntyre had chosen and he would work among some of the strongest and toughest men he could ever meet, and in time he too became one of them himself.

'The ship he was watchman on was a lot different from the coal- burners he sailed in' thought Jimmy this was oil-fired and clean in the boiler room, not like it was for him and his ship mates in days gone by. He was used to taking over the watch at four in the morning until eight o'clock four hours on and four off that's the way it was right through his voyages.

A man taking over would always have a quick look in front of the boiler to make sure the stoker he had taken over the watch from had left you enough coal to get you started, or there would be a few snide remarks made as he ascended the steel ladder up to the Fiddley to collect his washing before he made his way onto the open deck or to the focs'lehead to get his head down for a couple of hours.

Jimmy couldn't remember the number of times he would be looking up at the Pearson's water-level gauge to check the level was right, then a quick look at the steam pressure.

Sometimes the second engineer would have a look around then go on his way, when he was sure everything was ship-shape.

'Have you got a bit of 'black pan' for me and the lads?' If the cook had no uncooked meat on the table he would get a large joint of meat from the fridge and cut a chunk off. 'Here go and throw that into the furnace and don't come back' cook would say.

Jimmy would have a smile on his face as he descended the steel ladders from the Fiddley down to the boiler room.

The rest of the boiler room gang who would be on watch would be waiting in anticipation. When Jimmy produced the lump of raw meat, the smiles would be brighter than the fire in the furnace and out would come the special coal shovel that was used for cooking the bit of 'black pan'.

You could see your face in that shovel, it was always kept clean and polished. Every man would be excited seeing the meat put into the furnace on the shovel. A few minutes later out would come the steel shovel with the 'black pan', black as the hobs of hell, but cooked to the liking of every man in the stoke hold.

Jimmy McIntyre watchman now pulled the collar of his overcoat tight around his neck, as he looked over the side of the ship at the two cats down on the quay screeching at one another, their green eyes shining in the half light from the lamps on the dock shed. A confrontation was going on between the adversaries and it broke the quietness and the loneliness of the night for Jimmy. 'The two cats could have been two stokers having a disagreement' thought Jimmy.

A quick look over the side of the ship to make sure no-one was about and Jimmy would slip into Fiddley which was on top of the boiler room where the heat rose to warm his frail body. Many a time Jimmy with his ship mates would hang their washing in the Fiddley, the washing would be dry in a short time from the heat that rose above the boilers.

At about twelve o'clock midnight after making sure the coast was clear he would make his to the galley where he was sure to get something to eat off the cook if he was about, if not then the cook was sure to have left him something to drive the cold from his body. Jimmy got to thinking about how he would always stay friendly with the cook in his sea- going days and here he was still keeping in with the cook after his sea days were over.

Jimmy McIntyre was enjoying his beef sandwiches sitting in the warmth of the galley, his mind drifting back through the years and then on to today which came and went so quick; time had a way of speeding up these days he mused.

Jimmy's thoughts were still down in the boiler room, he

could remember how they would clean out the ashes from under the furnace, pulling them out with the steel rake, then shovelling them into forty-five gallon oil drums that would be standing on the steel plates. Once full a member of the crew would climb the ladder to the top of the boiler room, and send the winch cable down to hook onto the oil drums. The drums with their contents of ashes would be winched up to the top, then taken on deck where they would be dumped over the side of the ship.

'Well it could have been worse, at least I did see different aspects of life sailing abroad' thought Jimmy.

The cook had gone to bed and left Jimmy to lock the galley door when he had finished his tea and sandwiches. It was cold and damp outside on deck, but Jimmy was not the sort of man to sit around too long. He got to his feet ten minutes after the cook had left the galley, locked up and stepped over the 'combing' as he went through the doorway onto the deck and made his way to the gangway, where he looked over the side to see the same two wild cats still going at it hammer and tongs.

Jimmy McIntyre smiled when he thought about the cats. 'Not a worry in the world yet even they found something to fight over, one thing about them they kept the rat population down'. Without the wild cats the rats would take over.

Jimmy had a long night ahead of him until eight the next morning, a bit of a difference from four on and four off when he was at sea.

Four o'clock and the sound of a taxi pulling up at the gangway, it breaks the silence of the night, a young deck officer walks onto the top of the gangway leading a young woman down to the waiting taxi. 'Some things never change', thought Jimmy.

The night drew on, Jimmy sat on a bench at the top of the gangway looking up into the clear sky, not a cloud about. Jimmy smiled, looking up it's like a beautiful stage with the curtains drawn back showing the flickering lights of the stars, a vast expanse.

The sound of another taxi came to a halt at the bottom of the gangway, three crew members alighted from the cab, walked up the gangway like three silent players across the stage, oblivious to Jimmy's presence. 'A ship never sleeps, always got one eye open', thought Jimmy.

The long night was almost over, the light of a raw November day pushing its way through on the horizon.

Jimmy McIntyre signed the book, that would relieve him from his twelve-hour shift at the top of the gangway.

The cold air was still reverberating around Jimmy's neck as he pulled his collar tight.

A small dark object came into contact with Jimmy's foot as he was about to step onto the gangway. Looking down he would see two bright eyes and just hear a faint sound.

Jimmy picked the kitten up and looked at it. 'A wild cat you may be but you and me are going to be ship mates' he said.

As he wandered down the road to the room he occupied in the large old house in Seaforth he couldn't help but think that at the end of a hard working life all he ended up with was living in a single sad room with only a semi-wild cat as his main friend. Jimmy shrugged in his own philosphical way at his musings and walked down the road pushing the kitten inside his overcoat to keep it warm.

Pavement wares Highfield Street circa. 1900

Rosey

She hopped along the pavement and every few yards she would hop into the road. It was her build that attracted me to her. She was well groomed and had a lovely greyish look in her eyes, her legs were strong and firm and she was a fine looking specimen but something was not quite right. It did not seem right that such a good looking bird like her should be on her own.

Every time she hopped into the road she would venture further to the centre, getting closer to the traffic.

The hunger was getting the better of her, and she was becoming desperate.

Although the traffic on the road was light she still had to rise above the vehicles in order to avoid the oncoming danger. On closer inspection her wings seemed heavy and full of grime and every time she had to fly up to save herself from being crushed the effort was sapping her energy.

Rosey was not the sort of bird that you would normally see scavenging in the streets, she was a special kind of bird, a racing bird which had gone off course.

Rosey was feeling the cold, the hunger-pains were numbing her senses, and she was unable to fly any further until she found a few crumbs on the pavement or in the roadway to renew her energy. She would peck away at whatever she could see hoping she could digest something just to be able to get back in the air and fly to the safety of her loft where she would perch in peace with food and water in her belly, sleep would restore her strength to be able to clean her feathers and watch them come to life again.

The more Rosey had to jump about the more depressed she became, she had been cast out to fend for herself like the pigeons who live in the tops of warehouses or in the eaves of old buildings. Life expectancy among the common pigeons was much shorter than hers, but she was special, the thought of having to associate with these other birds made her depression all the harder to bear.

The traffic was building up on the road and the chances of searching for food were becoming more of an effort, her life was more in danger, her strength was rapidly draining from her, even the pavements were no longer safe. Silly school kids on the way home from school made things more of a burden by their constantly chasing her.

After what seemed like hours hopping around the pavement she came to rest in a gateway. She would have gone inside but the gate was closed and she didn't have the strength to fly over it; so she just huddled in the gateway.

November days are short and the light was starting to fade, she was feeling the cold and was utterly miserable.

Rosey's legs disappeared inside her feathers as she lay there huddled up, dejected and about to succumb to the damp November night, and the light going out for ever on her.

As she lay in a heap in the gateway another sad figure was making its way along the road towards Rosey, it was a drunken man. He was staggering from side to side his knees buckling under his weight but each time he was about to sink to the ground he would straighten up, then continue to repeat the same action over again.

The man had made way his way to the gateway, Rosey was not aware of him, his knees gave way, but before he straightened to put the spring back into his legs he noticed Rosey looking sad and frightened and unable to dodge out of his way, he swooped on Rosey his grimy hand spread across Rosey's back and he lifted her, turned her to face him. The man looked into Rosey's eyes, 'Hello lovely' he said. The sight of this human looking into her face made Rosey shake, she was helpless. Trapped inside of the big hand, Rosey could see his eyes were half closed but open enough for her to see the loneliness in the man's eyes, at least she thought that that was what it was. The man's gaze seemed to last forever, she hoped he would not drop her.

The sweat from the man's hands combined with the grime in her feathers would compress the wings to her body sending her crashing to the ground; as the fear was taking hold of Rosey the man's other hand came up level with Rosey's face. The hand opened up and straightened out, Rosey could see the broken biscuits as the man pushed them closer to her, the hunger got the better of her and she started to peck away at them, the pounding in her heart started to subside, she kept pushing the life saving food into her body.

The man with his big face was looking directly into Rosey's eyes, the fear that she had encountered was being taken over by the warmth she felt in her belly with the food starting to push her energy level up again.

The man was wearing a leather jacket with wide sleeves, and when Rosey had had her fill of biscuits he pulled down the zip on his jacket and trussed Rosey inside. She slid to the elbow of the sleeve where she was on her stomach and felt herself being swung in a cradle position every time the drunken man moved his elbow.

The darkness started to bring the fear back into Rosey's mind, she had been fed and felt nice and warm but what was to become of her now, how could she fly away now even though she was sure she had the energy to do so?

Rosey was going from one crisis to another, she felt just as trapped as ever.

The drunken man staggered on down the road, 'How are ya Rosey?' he would continue to whisper, passers-by would give the staggering man a wide berth.

'Are ya alright down there Rosey?'

A few more steps down the road and the drunken man would find sanctuary by pushing his back against a wall stretching it to expose his full height.

His left hand went under the right elbow that was cradling Rosey, then swinging both arms as if he was singing a child to sleep bursting into song.

Rosey, Rosey, don't be so dozy,
and have a good sleep
and have a good sleep.

And so he would go on until he staggered to the next wall or fence that would support his frame.

Poor Rosey was now truly in a state of panic, her feathers were all out of place, not a nice situation for a lady who had such a high standing in the pigeon world to find herself in; even the lower class of pigeon had more respect than she was getting. 'How to have your freedom', she would cry to herself.

Onward would go the drunken man, who looked much older than the years he had spent on this earth. Rosey was blind because she was trapped in her dark cell, but the young man was blind too with alcohol.

The drunken man came upon a shop with a bench in front of its window, displaying potted plants.

'Here ya are Rosey, look at this one', he said picking up one of the plants, 'How do you like that Rosey?' poking his head into his jacket. Rosey never answered, only the echo of his own voice could be heard in the confines of his leather jacket.

At last Rosey managed to get onto her side trying not to do harm to her feathers. She could see a streak of light coming through the elbow of the well-worn leather jacket. The light helped to take away some of the terror that Rosey felt incarcerated in the well-worn jacket elbow.

The drunken man placed the potted plant on the bench, picked up another, 'Do you like that Rosey?' holding the jacket open with the other hand, but taking care not to push the zip too far down.

Still talking to Rosey the drunken man started to move away from the front of the shop while still holding the potted plant.

The man had not moved more than a couple of yards when the shopkeeper, a very large man, grabbed the drunken man by the back of his collar, 'Come here you thieving bastard', he said.

Poor Rosey was feeling very sorry for herself trapped in the sleeve of the jacket. She was convinced she would never take to the air again, she was sure she would never see the waters of the English Channel between France and England, when taking part in a race.

Despair had set in, she could see no hope for herself, what an undignified position to be in laying on her side in the sleeve of an old sweaty jacket.

Rosey could hear a lot of shouting and she could feel herself being pushed from side to side, sliding up and down the sleeve. Every time she slid down the sleeve she hoped it would give way, but no such luck, it was fastened tightly at the man's wrist, so her prison gate stayed closed.

'Call the police', Rosey could hear the sound of voices becoming more violent.

The drunken man was being dragged backwards into the shop, 'Move and you are a dead man', said the shopkeeper.

'Let him go' said the shopkeeper's wife, 'It's only a potted plant, it's not worth much'.

'That's not the point, he is a shoplifter' he replied.

The drunken man tried to explain the situation he had found himself in.

'I'm sorry I never meant....' said the man.

'Shut up' said the shopkeper.

'But I....' said the drunken man.

'You can but I .... to the police', replied the shopkeper.

The shopkeeper was a large angry man with a roundish red face, the sort of face that would make you want to cross the road if it was heading towards you.

'Lock him in the back room until the police come', said the

red- faced man to his wife. 'If you move I will hit you over the head with a baseball bat'.

The red-faced man's anger was building up as he pushed the drunken man into the dark room and the shafts of light coming through the sleeves of the jacket were extinguished, leaving Rosey and the drunken man in total darkness.

The drunken man had now become a prisoner joining Rosey, cast in a dark cloak of fear and uncertainty as to what the future held for him.

After what seemed an eternity the door of the dark room opened letting in the light from the shop. In the doorway stood two policemen, 'Well what have we here?', one police officer said to the other.

The drunken man was in a very sorrowful state, his head down, but his arms were crossed, his left hand supporting the right elbow cradling Rosey.

'I am sorry I never meant to....', said the drunken man.

'I told you to shut your mouth', said the red-faced shop-keeper.

'OK sir', said the taller of the two policeme, 'We'll take care of things now'.

The red-faced man was disappointed that he could not come out with a mouth full of obscenities to be directed towards the dejected captive.

Rosey thought it best to stay quiet while all the talk was going on.

'What's this man done sir?', said the smaller of the two policemen.

'He stole a potted plant', replied the shopkeeper.

'But he....', said the shopkeeper's wife.

'Be quiet woman', said the red-faced man, 'I will do the explaining'.

'Yes go on sir', said one of the policemen, casting a glance and a smile towards his colleague.

'Did you say he stole a potted plant sir?' said the policeman.

'Yes' said the shopkeeper.

'Then could you tell me where the potted plant was when this man lifted it?'

'Outside on the bench with the other plants', said the woman.

'I told wou woman', said the shopkeeper.

'No sir, please let your wife go on', said the policeman.

'Yes it was outside'.

'And what happened?', said the taller of the policemen.

'The man picked it up and staggered away with it'.

'And what did you do sir?' said the policeman turning to the shopkeeper.

'I dragged him back and locked him in there'.

'How much is the plant worth?'

'Fifty pence' said the woman.

'Can't we let him go if he pays for it?', the woman was clearly embarrassed.

'I want him prosecuted' said the shopkeeper.

The drunken man had taken some money from his pocket and tried to push it towards the woman.

'It's too late for that now, we will have to take you in' said one of the policemen.

The red-faced man had a smirk on his face, his wife held her head low, as the dejected drunken man walked out of the door the two policemen by his side.

Rosey could hear the drone of the car engine. She was more calm and lay very quiet in an upright position.

The two policemen started to laugh. 'Sorry mate, to think we have to take you in for a potted plant', a smile came to the face of the drunken man, he started to see the funny side of his situation.

The man felt much more calm in himself knowing that the threat of violence towards him was no longer present.

Rosey felt the police car come to a stop and the leather jacket sleeve being lifted into a bent position as the drunken man raised himself from the seat of the police car, the sound of marching feet, then a sudden stop, the sound of new voices penetrated the leather sleeve.

The drunken man was still unsteady on his feet standing at the desk of the police station.

Rosey still chose to remain quiet, a lot of talking was taking place between Rosey's captor and the policemen.

The drunken man started to move, then the sound of the jacket zip being pulled, filled Rosey's frail body with hope, then without any warning the man's arm slipped out of the jacket sleeve.

A gushing sound reverberated through the jacket as it glided to the floor of the police station. Rosey came down with a bump as she landed in a not very dignified position, the jacket engulfed her pinning her to the floor.

The jacket was discarded but Rosey was still a prisoner.

The drunken man was shepherded into a cell, the heavy door shut behind him, Rosey lay on the floor outside of the cell.

Rosey was not only a prisoner in the jacket she was also incarcerated within a police station along with her captor.

After what seemed like hours Rosey still lay on the floor of the police station, not a sound coming from her body. Hunger was taking over from the fear, and despair had set in once again for Rosey, her position was hopeless, not a nice situation for a dignified lady.

Rosey could see in her mind, the loft owner waiting for her to return. She could picture him looking into the sky waiting for his prize racing pigeon to return, what if he could see her now, he would probably disown her.

The sound of the cell door opening and voices startled Rosey, she tried to lift herself into a sitting position but the weight of the jacket still kept her pinned down.

Voices were loud and clear for a few seconds but then faded away leaving Rosey in a dark silent world once again.

The drunken man seemed more steady on his feet as he walked towards the desk in the reception area of the police station minus his jacket.

Hours of sitting alone in the cell without drink sobered him up a little.

So much time had elapsed since, the drunken man had forgotten about Rosey lying in a heap on the police station floor outside of the cell.

The sergeant at the desk gave the man his personal items back, items he had taken from him before placing him in the cell.

The man was making his way to the open door when one of the policemen shouted to him, 'Your coat is outside the cell door'.

The man dragged his coat from the door and out flew Rosey, up towards the ceiling her energy restored, she was almost free and not letting the chance for freedom go.

In the meantime the policemen in the station could not contain their amusement at the sight of Rosey escaping from the leather jacket.

'Have you got a rabbit in that jacket also?' cried one policeman in a fit of laughter.

Rosey did not stay to find out, her outstretched wings took her to freedom through the open doors of the police station.

An interested group in Harding Street. circa. 1934

The Apple Orchard

Simon's mind was in turmoil lying on his back in the ambulance, the pain from his leg surging through his body like red hot coals, the broken leg gave a floating sensation each time the ambulance drove over an uneven stretch of road.

The ambulance men had done their best to make him comfortable, and he was the sort of man who let the crew of the ambulance know of his gratitude.

Simon always had respect for medical people whether it be a porter or surgeon, but he felt only resentment towards himself for climbing an unsafe ladder while painting the front of his house.

A lifetime in the building trade should have taught him better, but no, he was the wise one who acted like a fool, how many times had he told young men never to climb an unsteady ladder but then doesn't this only go to prove the point that accidents are always awaiting the unwary.

The pain was still coming in waves, but it did not stop the negative thoughts that Simon directed towards himself as he drifted in and out of a semi-conscious state.

The ambulance was making good time, but it seemed like a never ending journey.

The ambulance came to a stop in front of the casualty doors of the City Hospital.

Simon was transferred to a waiting trolley and taken into the casualty department.

The pain from the leg was so severe Simon's senses seemed to fuse together, time seemed to lose all meaning.

He looked up at a nurse helping to push the trolley, 'What's happening nurse?' he said.

The leg had been twisted in the fall resulting in a very bad fracture.

Simon could remember being told to count to ten by one of the staff in the theatre. Back in the bed in the ward, lying on his back, he smiled when he felt the plaster cast stretching the length of his leg. 'Well that will stop your gallop mate, you are not going very far in this state'.

As the mist cleared from his brain, Simon started to look at his surroundings, the long Victorian ward was familiar, 'Yes this could be the one I was in all those years ago. It seemed a lifetime ago. I can remember I must have been about nineteen and she was the same age'.

The curtain of mist that had clouded Simon's mind had lifted and the memories that were so implanted in his mind started to return.

Jean, how could I forget her, she must have been the first girl I fell in love with, I was in the bed at the top end of the ward, it could have been this one or one very like it, the door led out onto a path that took you up to a little apple orchard, but I doubt if that little orchard is still there.

Jean, how *could* I forget her. The times she would tease me when I was feeling sorry for myself. I suppose just the way I am now, but this time there is no Jean.

Simon was delving into his memory in the same way a man could be looking for the right books in a library to give him the right answers.

I was very ill when I came into this ward or one like it, Jean was one of those wonderful members of staff that helped put the life back into me. I can still remember that she was doing exams and hoping to become an S.R.N. I wasn't sure what that meant but I think it was State Registered Nurse, yes, I think that was what S.R.N. means.

Simon, lay flat on his back, his eyes exploring every corner of the ward, could see Jean walking towards him when she could snatch a few minutes to herself. She would sit on the side of the bed and talk to him.

He smiled, yes that is how it started. She took away the pain and boredom of the months of hospitalisation. She gave him the reason to live. I fell in love with a dream, or an angel. I am not sure which.

The funny thing is I can just see her now walking down the ward, her dark brown hair carefully concealed within her cap she was about five foot six. She was slim and could gather a good pace when walking the length of the ward. I would waken every morning to see that lovely smile, and the days she was not on duty my heart would sink.

Simon had been in hospital for a couple of weeks, and his mind was still recalling his dream. Jean, maybe she was only a dream or perhaps an angel who came to comfort me.

No, Jean was real all right, but why did she pick on me? She could have found better than me to walk in the apple orchard with.

My God! I had a low opinion of myself, I was without an education and came from very poor surroundings and yet she fell in love me and I with her.

Throughout my life I have lived with her vision coming to me always when I least expected it.

She could not have been happy, she was engaged to be married when we met, yet her feelings were as strong for me as mine for her.

I had Jean on a pedestal, never a bad thought could enter my head towards her, we were both nineteen, my thoughts were pulled towards her.

Did she marry the man she was engaged to? I always felt she did. In those days if you were engaged you did the expected thing, you got married, the trouble was it was not always the right thing to do.

A sadness came to Simon's face while lying there he was totally engrossed in his thoughts for Jean.

It was after discharge from hospital all those years ago, that we tried to get together. I can still remember the cinema we went to, we arranged to meet outside the Bank just down the road from where she lived.

I stood outside the Bank for what seemed an eternity, I was clutching a leather shoulder bag that had been carefully wrapped by my older sister.

I had laboured making the bag during my long stay in hospital, I prayed that Jean would like it.

My heart raced as I saw Jean making her way towards me, my lack of education and humble beginnings were taking their toll on me, being so young I felt that I was not worthy of her, I was ashamed of myself.

It puzzled me to know what attraction Jean could find in me but here we were climbing together onto the local bus on the journey to the cinema.

Although I watched the images on the cinema's screen they conveyed very little to me, my mind was filled with the beauty of the lady who sat by my side. I can feel the warmth of her gentle hand as I held it in mine.

The day passed all too soon, it was soon time to say goodbye to Jean as she left she said, 'write to me Simon and I shall let you know when I am off duty'.

I thought my heart would break as I saw her walk away from me, I wanted to rush after her to hold her in my arms and never let her go.

Perhaps my own ignorance at not being able to express my thoughts, hence my silence, made my beloved Jean think I had forgotten about her but I never could.

After many weeks of boredom lying in his hospital bed Simon was glad to be going home even though he was a widower and his children had all flown the nest. He still had his little business that filled the empty void in his life. Over the years Simon had not only built up a sound business, he had also achieved a moderate education although it was a hard slog.

After all the goodbyes to the other patients in the ward and the thanks paid to the staff, Simon was given a lift home by ambulance. His leg would still need some rest before he would be fully mobile.

He was given some help to get into the ambulance by its crew. and he thanked them and made himself comfortable for the journey home.

'Hope you don't mind' said the driver to Simon, 'We're giving this nurse a lift, she is going the same way as you. Okay Sister, hop in and you can hold Simon's hand on the way home' he joked.

Simon looked at the Sister when she sat down. 'I'll be doing a bit of hopping for a while', he said 'What would we do without people like you and the ambulance crews to look after us' he added.

The nursing sister did not reply, she just kept looking at Simon. As they looked at one another the years gently rolled away and they both remembered the walks to the orchard and hours spent together all those years ago.

Simon reached out for Jean's hand as she asked rather tentatively 'Will your wife be waiting for you when you get home? You will need help for some time'.

'I have no wife' said Simon softly.

'Well, you will need some help', continued Jean. 'It's you, I can hardly believe it, it's you. I have thought of no-one but you, since I have been here', Jean smiled, 'Like I said, Simon, you are going to need somebody to look after you'.

Simon glanced down and noticed Jean did not wear a ring on her left hand, Simon smiled, and with the slightest tear in his eyes said, 'you know, Jean, wouldn't it have been wonderful if we had had a lift in this ambulance those many years ago'.